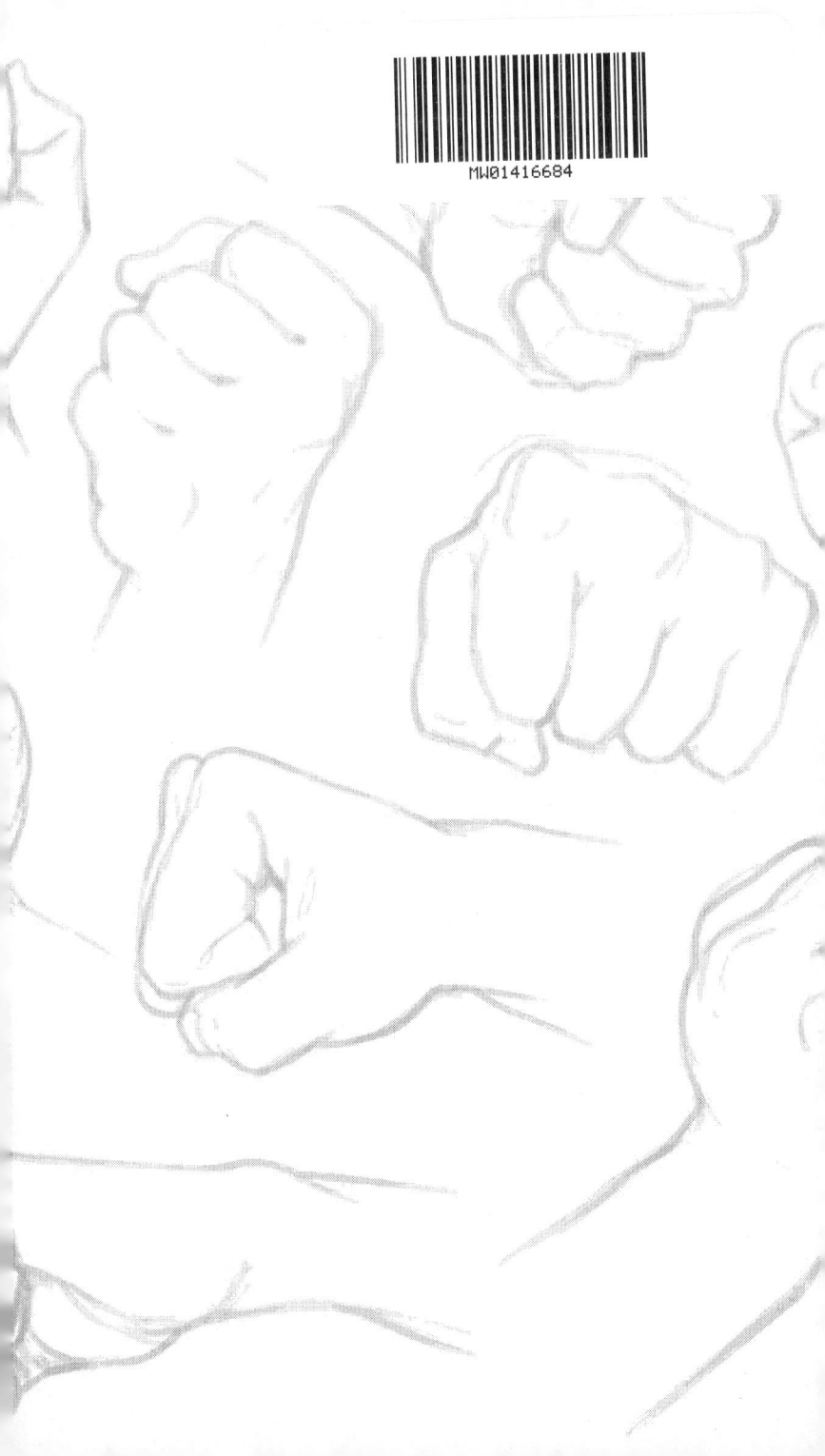

BEGGARS BALL THEIR FISTS

OTHER WORKS BY TODD SHERMAN

Pitching Ice Cubes at the Sun: A Book of the Dead

Opals for Libras

Kong Hong

Paralytic States

Fluid Babies

Rise, Osiris!

Phlogistics of a Simple Man

Obscurdities

Stygian Blue

Begorrah Bone House

He Grasps the Heel

Toxic Nightjars

Bark Your Shins

People Our Solitude

Primaeval Daemons

Poached Eggs in Aspic

In So Bright a World

Malapriapism

A Still Lustrous Eye

Available in paperback and ebook on amazon.com

OR

QUESTIONS WITH UNSATISFYING ANSWERS

BY TODD SHERMAN

Copyright ©2024 Todd Sherman
All Rights Reserved

Cover Art, Interior Art, Layout & Design:
Melissa Hindle-Sherman

Editing:
Ninth House Editing

ISBN: 9798327701861

To all of us beggars.

...CONTENTS...

11. WHY THE PATRIOT PARTY IS SO FREAKING AWESOME

65. WHAT BECAME OUR GREATER PURPOSE

87. WHERE THE COOL KIDS GO IN NEW BRAXTON OR DOVERTON

109. WHO COSGROVE SAW

121. WHOM WE MEANT TO KILL

135. WHY THE ANCIENT EGYPTIANS REMOVED BRAINS THROUGH THE NOSTRILS

143. WHAT WAS IN THE BOX BY THE SIDE OF THE ROAD

165. WHEN THEY DIED

179. HOW I KNOW I'M NOT A GOD

193. WHAT THAT SOUND WAS

217. WHAT MATTERS TO US

WHY THE PATRIOT PARTY IS SO FREAKING AWESOME

For God and country, someone once said, but we can't remember who. Or can we?

Was it you?

It wasn't me, Ricky Limes said.

Was it you?

Dim Junham shakes his head.

Not me.

Was it you, Mr. Ridicoloso?

No way, he said. It wasn't me.

Peeps, the Frogman of Doom, coughs into his fist.

I think it was Hitler, he said, not looking anyone in the eyes.

No way, no how, said Wilt Corley. Why rush to Hitler already?

Because he's going to fix the country, Ricky said.

Hitler?

Who? Oh, no. I thought you were talking about Trump.

Whoa. Trump's miles apart from Hitler.

Wilt spread his arms to illustrate this fact.

Hecks to the yeah, Dim Junham said.

Oh, yeah, of course.

Ricky Limes was speaking nervously since he most likely realized just at that moment he'd spoken outside of what the circle would accept.

Mr. Ridicoloso ribbed Ricky for being a foreigner. He hailed from some Central or South American country that all the members in the circle failed at pointing out correctly on a map.

To be fair, the map Wilt had pinned to the Corleys' household wall was of America, the only country that warranted the cost of ink and paper, apparently. This map of America was beside an eighty-five-inch TV. It was a big wall. It was a bigger house.

Now, now, Wilt said. Ricky can't help it he was born in Colombia.

Nicaragua.

Yeah, whatever. Wilt thumbed back to his map. We're in America now, buddy.

That's right, Dim said.

Darn skippy, said no one, but maybe everyone felt it.

Just joking, Mr. Ridicoloso said. We love the crap out of you, Ricky.

That's right, Dim said again, since repeating himself with slightly different inflection was his favorite thing to do when not pontificating about the libs.

WHY THE PATRIOT PARTY IS SO FREAKING AWESOME

Yeah, Peeps the Frogman of Doom said. And I was only joking about the reference to Hitler.

Well, to be fair, Dim Junham said, not all his ideas were bad.

There hung a moment of silence. Some maybe nodded. Some definitely shuffled their feet. No one dared raise the specter of Hitler again, not even to make a disparaging remark about vegetarians.

Wilt Corley broke that silence with a tack hammer:

Where we go one, we go all.

Where we go one, we go all, the rest said.

So . . .

Yeah . . .

The reason we're here . . .

For God and country.

For God and country, they repeated, and so Dim Junham said it a third time.

Wilt scratched his beefy chest since it had the girth and round shininess of a cow's flank in the naked sunlight.

He scratched it again while everyone waited for him to speak since, we guess, he was their leader.

He's the leader, right? no one asked.

We bet Wilt wouldn't know the difference between a tack or a ball-peen hammer if either one had struck him on his broad skull. Like a reflex, he cracked that skull to say:

So, I know I'm not alone in this when I say that I don't like the direction the country is going in and that direction is as crooked as crooked can be. They say the road to evil is wide and paved with good intentions, but we need to narrow the field, I say, and I think you'll all agree, that narrowing the field to the best of what America can be is the best thing for America right now.

I couldn't have said it better myself, Dim said, even if it were a thing I would've said.

Everyone nodded. We think Ricky Limes went along just to keep in motion with the rest of the group. We're not entirely certain that Ricky, being a foreigner from uncertain Spanish-speaking parts, even understood what Wilt Corley had said.

We mean to say, would anyone understand Wilt Corely outside this group? We're outside the group and we're straight flummoxed.

I understand what you're saying, Mr. Ridicoloso said. I mean, we don't want to become Nazis, and we're dangerously close to that happening with the way things are going.

Peeps the Frogman of Doom peeped up with a finger held aloft, unwetted and sensing no breeze within the room.

Uhhh, are we on Hitler again?

Not like Eva Braun was, Dim said, nudging at empty air since no one of flesh was close enough for him to nudge. I mean, am I right?

Good one, someone said, and it didn't matter who; take it from us.

Yeah, I agree, Ricky Limes said, that was a good one.

Um, do you even know who Eva Braun was? Peeps said.

Was? Ricky said. Why, did she die?

Wait? Who was Eva Braun?

Wilt Corley had said this. There wasn't a hint of irony in the statement since a growing fascistic regime is often unconscious of fascism growing, or even of the meaning of irony. He also may have been surprised to learn that Hitler had been a vegetarian and that it wasn't a bit of fake news fobbed off by the mainstream media. Much like he would've been absolutely floored to hear about how sick Hitler had gotten when he'd visited a concentration camp at a MAGA event.

Maybe it hadn't happened. More hands off, pulling down the train blinds, cracking a Fanta while reading regular reports from SS task forces. And Wilt's brain would undoubtedly explode at how similar the words "tourniquet" and "eternity" sound from a distance.

Wilt Corley's running definition of irony was far closer to the meaning of coincidence. But, then again, so is most people's, running or otherwise.

Only Communists and their sympathizers knew the difference. The Reds, the pinko bastards. No one uttered this last statement since all five members in this slowly accreting molecule of purported greatness never employed expletives. The Bible had said something about this, about swearing to God, they'd swear, or some crap.

We know the exact passage that refers to this, but we're keeping mum since we believe this group should do their own damn research. As should you.

All these paragraphs following Wilt's question as to the identity of Eva Braun were meant, in part, to illustrate the depth of silence that had ensued after that question. Even Wilt must've sensed how far off that narrow path they'd strayed. He hadn't quite spoken his piece, even if that piece was anything except an actual peace, and so had spread out his arms again.

Anyway, he said, let's get this back to how we're going to fix things.

Did something break? Ricky Limes said.

Wilt clamped his hands together and breathed a beefy sigh.

Yes, Ricky. America. America's broke.

America is broke?

Peeps the Frogman of Doom chimed in, this time with his finger not aloft, but stuck to his hand with the other fingers and shoved into the front right pocket of his American-made jeans.

Broken. America is broken. If it were broke, we would owe people money.

Uhhh . . .

China, nobody said, but they sure as heck were all thinking it. Or Jina, more likely, since that was the circle's private joke that they'd appropriated from other circles. Chinggis Khan's not laughing. Neither are the guys before Homo Sapiens Sapiens, the Neander Talls, since they were all killed off, or had been assimilated, or were caught in Hindenburg-sized icebergs, despite their advantage in height.

America first, Dim Junham said. Remember, guys? America first.

Nods. Shuffles. Thumbs toward maps. Well, one thumb and one map.

Where we go one, we go all.

Where we go one, we go all, everyone else said.

So, how are we going to go about it?

Well, Peeps, Wilt said. That's why we're here.

Why are we here? Ricky Limes asked.

He'd been looking up, maybe looking for the hand of God to write the answer they'd sought to the hard white plaster of Wilt Corley's Wyoming-sky-wide ceiling.

Even though America's pretty good, Ricky, in fact great, Wilt went on, it could be greater, it could be as great as it once was, greater than it ever had been even, and greater still once we help get the ship righted on the narrow road I was talking about earlier.

Wilt closed an eye and bored deeply into Ricky's forehead with the open one.

You understand what I'm saying here, Ricky?

What a condescending cow, one of us said. Move over move it or lose it move your illusion move on move on move on to greener cow-pied pastures.

Sí, sí. God with us.

Yes, surely, Ricky. We want God on our side.

For God and country.

If God be for us, Dim said, who can be against? I mean, who would dare be against us?

No one. No one and nobody.

Amen and amen.

Not amen and awomen.

Don't get us started on the First Amendment with the government not establishing a religion or limiting the free expression thereof as interpreted by the Supreme Court as the basis for the separation of church and state and how odd it is that Conservatives got their boxer briefs in a twist over amen and awomen when somehow it's okay to violate the first amendment to the US Constitution and endorse a prayer before a governmental meeting.

What's the first order of business?

Dim Junham would love to be the leader since he so often acts like one, at least acting like a man who's attained some semblance of wisdom, even if that man is more properly a follower of a leader in an ill-fitting suit. He's wearing that suit now. No one else present is wearing a suit.

It would pain Wilt Corley to be forced to wear a suit, let alone a mask.

And it would pain us, too, to see it since Wilt Corley in a suit is the closest he'll ever come to doing what's expected, to outfitting himself like a leader, even if it's only on Sundays to kneel before a hovering vision of the Holy Ghost on the megachurch's projection screen.

The first order of business, Wilt said, is what to name our party.

I thought we were going to be called the Patriot Party?

Mr. Ridicoloso looked about as confused as a ridiculous man can when not presently conscious of how ridiculous his name is.

WHY THE PATRIOT PARTY IS SO FREAKING AWESOME

The Patriot Party was formed in the 60s by poor white people fighting against racism, of all things, in their communities and actually supported by the black power movement of the time.

This from Peeps. Of course a fallout ensued, always ensuing, never fully falling out before an event since that wouldn't lend itself to handy tautology. Internet memes don't make themselves.

What the heck are you going on about?

Sí, sí.

Yeah, I say, yeah.

I propose, Wilt said, scratching his broad beefy chest, we go by simply Patriot Party.

Peeps was shaking his head.

That's what I said. There's already been the Patriot Party.

Wilt shook his head even more emphatically.

No. There'll be no 'the' in the name.

What?

Sounds good to me, Dim said.

Mr. Ridicoloso was beaming.

Sounds great.

Sounds like America's going to be great again, Ricky said.

Peeps the Frogman of Doom took his finger back from his pocket and popped it into the breezeless air.

Um. The initials would be PP, though.

Oh . . .

Yeah . . .

That don't sound good.

There was a clearing of a wide beefy chest and that's how it's known that that chest belonged to one Wilt Corley, which initialism would make him WC or water closet for short. Pee-pee, indeed.

Okay, then, how about the . . .

The what?

Worm-baited breath.

Those oh-so-tender hooks.

Wilt Corley would never get our jokes.

Old Patriots Organization, then, Wilt said.

Even though he said it, he surely didn't seem satisfied with it. In fact, it appeared as if he were grabbing words from that stale air and simply setting them on each other's heels. Sans-serif. Call the sheriff. An eternity of tourniquets. Wilt didn't even scratch at his chest. Maybe best to move on to a better party name, his face had said if his face could be said to utter anything of sense.

It's got 'old' in the title, Mr. Ridicoloso said. That kind of sucks.

Well, so does your nom de plume, Peeps said.

Your what?

Don't get all Frenchie on us.

Leave it to a Frogman to get all French on us.

Dim done repeated some dumb one else this time.

Ridicoloso is my real name.

It is?

And my name's not Ricky Limes.

We know that, Ricky.

Uh . . . my name's not really Dim.

Peeps the Frogman of Doom rolled his wet eyes.

Yeah, Dim, we know you just inverted your name. Like Wilt Corley over there.

Hey, hey, hey. Let's get this back on the Appropriated Patriot Party, Wilt said.

And off Eva Braun, Peeps muttered.

WAIT.

What is the Appropriated Patriot Party?

Ahem.

Well, Dim, I'm glad you asked. And for the opportunity to also answer Mr. Ridicoloso, who I can see is just chomping at the bit like Pac-Man chomps on ghosts.

How many ghosts would a Pac-Man chomp if a Pac-Man could chomp ghosts?

I could live with APP, Peeps said. I guess.

Me, too.

Wasn't that a movement about women being raped? Ricky asked.

What?

Move on. We bet a 'no' means a 'yes' to these guys.

But why 'appropriated?'

Wilt blinks his eyes enough times for it to set his hand in motion and that hand's motion is making a left to right across his chest, nails inward, passing and repassing until everyone in the room felt as if they, too, had been just as perfectly itchy.

'Cause we're taking it back.

Duh, Dim said to Peeps.

A-freaking-men.

It's about time.

Someone's got to stand up for the white guy in these troubled times.

And against:

Handouts.

Cancel culture.

The Red wave.

Illegals.

The woke mob.

Stupid snowflakes.

The cultural elite.

Ground Zero mosques.

Socialism.

Climate change.

Mommy's basement.

We will not rest, Wilt said, until every migrant that doesn't even speak English, unlike good old Ricky Limes here who doesn't insult us with his Mexican, I say that every comrade who comes here and pretends he's a patriot with his talk of sustainable development and safe spaces and jamming global warming down our throats, I say, we will not rest until we take our country back and own the libs for once and for all until all the God-blessed American people can sleep free from sea to shining sea. Amen.

Um.

Peeps the Frogman of Doom doesn't have a beefy chest to scratch. He's got a finger, just that one finger for emphasis, and he's painfully aware, just now, how insignificant that sole finger is within Wilt Corley's sprawling family room.

Peeps doesn't say anything.

Silence ensues.

Somewhere on a Sunday a megachurch or amphitheater or stadium will have a projection screen for an eyepatch, and they'll all see the same thing, we'll all see the same thing, until the thing is the only true thing spoken in a meaningless litany, and yet, always believed for it's never questioned.

I went to see him personally, we could hear someone say, which is the same thing as a hot water heater or an evening sunset or frozen ice or the dilapidated ruins of the United States of America that's been given away free on the summit at the top of the mountain around 2 PM in the afternoon in close proximity to a dry desert.

Or so we've heard it with our own ears. It's adequate enough. As an added bonus, a dark-haired brunette will come to you with the necessary requirement of predictions of the future. And we'll all know and we'll all know for sure and we won't have to ask anybody since we've done the research. The verdict may still be out on the science, but we'll know. Oh, we'll know. Or they'll know, we mean.

What a sad misfortune.

It is what it is, Dim said.

If I perish, I perish, Peeps said.

Just make sure they prepay in advance, Mr. Ridicoloso said. We don't want any freeloaders.

Take turns, Ricky said, nodding. One after the other.

There's a pause. A really long pause, without a finger of protest. A pause as long as Wilt's family room is wide.

You'll know it's true when we say that we heard it with our own ears:

Where we go one, we go all.

Where we go one, we go all, of course the rest say.

Wouldn't it be effing awesome, though?

Mr. Ridicoloso is asking it of everyone, and no one knows to what he's referring.

There's a scampering sound, like teeth lightly biting at tile. It's the dog. Wilt Corley's family dog. He's got something between the jaws of his heavy dog's body. That something protruding from canine lips is a hard metal thing and it isn't a finger.

Whoa!

It's a gun. A handgun. A handgun in the very real mouth of the Corley's family dog, padding about on the bamboo floor.

Lucky!

Whoa, hey there, Lucky!

Lockheed, come here.

Wilt bends down, greets the family dog at dog level, and extracts the family gun from the dog's mouth.

Did you say 'Lockheed?'

It is Lockheed.

It's not Lucky?

Who's Lucky?

We all are, I'd say, Peeps the Frogman of Doom said. He could've bit down on the trigger and sent a bullet into the chest — or shin, rather — of a member of the Appropriated Patriot Party.

Peeps was doing a poor job of covering his own shins with all his fingers.

It's good, it's cool, Wilt said. Right, Lockheed?

Why's the dog's name Lockheed?

It's only appropriate that Mr. Ridicoloso would be the one taken aback by how ridiculous a dog name Lockheed is.

He wasn't the only one, apparently.

I mean, Dim said, is the family cat named Martin?

Holy poop.

Wilt Corley had never considered this. Or had he? We know him to not be the most truthful, the most self-examining, of persons.

The dog padded away. Wilt would've stowed the gun in his belt, but his gut was too Texan big, so he instead laid it upon the mantle beside his wife's vintage cookbooks and porcelain knickknacks. Cookbooks in the family room? The family that eats together stays together, we guess.

> With a knick knack paddy whack give a dog a gun.

Stand your ground, Peeps said.

Where we go dog, we go all, no one said.

Dim Junham said something, and then he said it again.

Mr. Ridicoloso agreed.

Ricky Limes complied, since he was used to compliance when living in that Communist South or Central American country.

Donde va uno, vamos todos.

Peeps let his naked finger hit naked air but held his tongue.

Wilt, oh, Wilt. He opened his mouth and words just gushed out:

I'll fly away, oh Lord, I'll fly away. Oh, I'll fly awaaaay!

Where we go one.

We go all.

Wilt's actual words, though, were:

Hungry like a wolf.

No. A lion, if anything. It's on the letterheads, if letterheads were a thing that the Appropriated Patriot Party would use.

So then, Wilt's total and true and unfakenews words were:

Stop. Spreading. Rumors!

Oh, the irony.

Looks like the NRA got kicked out of Jersey, of course, Wilt said. Leave it to the Lefties to screw up something as simple as guns. I mean, it's easy: they're for protection, they're for fun, they're a big part of what's kept America great all these years, even if it's in a bit of a slump now, with Sleepy Joe snoozing through the Communist meetings.

Wilt bent down to pet his dog, but the family dog had padded away. Instead, Wilt stood up with a groan and a couple of gunshot cracks. He's got a big heart, after all, and that huge muscle pumps fifty-gallon drums of blood, and that sweet crude runs its fungible essence to every capillary and corpuscle within manifested destiny, from coast to coast, from C to shining C.

Sea to shining sea, boys, Wilt said, bracing himself against the mantle.

What's that?

Ricky Limes wants to know since he hasn't memorized "America the Beautiful" or the national anthem or the Constitution or its amendments or the entire menu of Taco Bell. But then, who's got time for all that?

It's America, Ricky. Wilt clamps his meaty hands. It's all of ours.

Manifest Destiny, Dim Junham said, nodding. Our grand destiny is obvious and writ by the finger of God.

Wilt nodded along, still bracing himself so he wouldn't fall with his enthusiasm.

And if New Jersey won't have them, he said, I say the NRA can good and well come here to the great state of Texas.

It could be Texas. It could be Wyoming. It could be Alabama or Alaska or the flaccid dripping penis of Florida. The state doesn't matter. It just needs to be a space big enough for hearts that thump with patriot pride and the pioneering spirit and the lust for more land more land since more houses on that land meant more walls for eighty-five-inch TVs, family portraits in matching sweatshirts, and the gun rack or safe or appropriated umbrella stand (wherever guns are kept when they're not winking in the sun).

Wilt Corley gushed on:

Every red-blooded American can find a home here, free of cancel culture and queer TV, where a man can be a man and a woman can be a woman and there's no one to give them crap about it, where everything's deep-fried since everything tastes better deep-fried (everyone nodded), and where the deep state can't get its pink eco-fingers in our pies, in our homes we've worked so hard to build (none of them had built their homes), in our churches that proclaim the one great religion since it's the only true religion, and I bet the NRA gives us all a great big Texan pat on the back.

A new gun would be nice, Mr. Ridicoloso said.

We getting new guns?

No, Ricky. Dim crimps his lips and slowly shakes his hairless head. It's a metaphor, buddy. A meh-tah-fore. Get it?

Ricky Limes smiles and nods enthusiastically, but it's clear he's not paying proper attention since he's pointing at a picture on the Corley's mantle of the Corley family in identical red sweatshirts.

What's Covid Christmas?

Wilt turns his big body toward the mantle.

Oh, that. He smiles as wide as a picket fence. That was our joke, since we couldn't spend Christmas out like we usually do, free of fake news about the virus, and holed up at the ole homestead instead, with matching shirts, 'cause it's funny. You know?

Ricky nodded but his face flashed consternation. He didn't smile and he didn't own a picket fence.

The Christmas-light font's a nice touch, Dim said.

Yeah, that was the wife's idea.

Why is the one girl wearing a mask in the photo?

Mr. Ridicoloso pointed his meaty finger, but it wasn't quite as meaty as Wilt Corley's.

That's my son's girlfriend. Wilt's smile dropped for a second, but only for a second. She's a bit of a Lefty, but we're working on her. You know, if it becomes serious then things will have to change.

Amen, Dim said.

And awomen, Ricky added.

No one laughed.

Right, right? Is funny, right?

Still no one laughed.

So, she wore the mask the whole time?

Mr. Ridicoloso had never stopped pointing.

No, no, Wilt said. Like I said, we're working on her. We made a joke of it, like with our matching shirts, and she got tired of defending it, so she gave it up.

Like the ghost?

What? No, no, Ricky. Nothing like that.

Mr. Ridicoloso nodded and dropped his hand with the pointer finger. He curled that finger into a loose fist and tapped the bottom of it against a palm.

That's it, that's the way, he said. You got to wear them down, keep at them until they just throw up their hands and say, screw it, okay, okay.

That's right, Wilt said.

But would she give up her ghost?

Dim looked annoyed. No, Ricky. No one died.

Except for six hundred thousand to COVID, Peeps the Frogman of Doom muttered.

Silence reigned. It could've been raining, literally, in the Corleys' rolling plain of a living room and no one would've peeped a word. Wilt Corley, though, never the man to admit defeat, opened his big mouth again and let his freshly painted picket fence go on gleaming.

Wilt jammed his hands into his denim pockets. There was barely enough room for the tips of his fingers.

Well, as for me and my house, he said, we will serve the Lord.

Amen, Dim said.

Where we go one, we go all? Ricky dared.

Yes, yes, Ricky. That's it. That's it exactly.

Dim patted Ricky Limes on his skeletal back. He could well and truly fit inside of Wilt's wide frame. Ricky, not Dim. Dim could barely fit in his own skin.

We guess all Texans are built big. Like their toast and National beers and great white star on their lonely flag.

If the Appropriated Patriot Party is indeed in Texas. We don't think they hold to any one state. Their ideology is LEGION and that Gadarene tribe needed room, lots of space, without competing ideologies to muck up the vista.

Untrimmed doggie claws on the bamboo again.

Lucky! Good boy, Lucky.

It's Lockheed, Ricky, Peeps the Frogman of Doom said. He ate Martin the cat and is now having a go with Wilt's slipper.

Lockheed had a brown leather slipper in its friendly jaws.

Wilt bent down with a groan and a pop of his knee. He went to that knee so he wouldn't fall over. He held out his hand to the mouth that wouldn't bite him for that mouth was always full of gun or slipper or family cat.

What you got there, buddy?

He retrieved the slipper. Something fell out of it. A gray plastic block that was meant to be snapped to something much larger.

Oh, wow, Wilt said. You found it, Lockheed.

What is it?

Dim scratched at his shining scalp.

It's the missing piece to the Death Star.

Excuse me?

Lockheed barked.

That's right, buddy. That's right.

Wilt rubbed down the dog with his left hand while holding the LEGO piece with his right.

You have a Death Star?

Ricky Limes hunted the circle of faces for an answer. The answer, for him, wasn't there. The answer couldn't be read in wrinkles or jowls. A beggar clasping and unclasping his hand at legal tender that would never be proffered.

Legal Texan tender. The Alamo in green in the background. Money for the confederates. Or maybe they were in Farmington, Connecticut. Or New Britain. Somewhere in the border between the two, possibly. Or it could've been simply a Connecticut-sized hole in the laboring lung of Texas.

Who could say in which state one would breathe more freely? Which part of which state? Gulf or desert or plains? The Berkshires or whaling coasts? Ideology, like money, moves along these state lines and makes a home where it will.

We know it doesn't really matter where that home is. Confederates are the same everywhere. Only the accents and climates are different.

Wilt stood up. Lockheed barked again and turned and toenails clipped along the smooth and wide wooden floor.

This little beggar's been nagging me a while, he said. I can't believe it was in my slipper the whole time.

No one else in the circle could believe it, either. No one could believe Wilt's luck. No one could believe his lucky dog's luck in finding the missing piece to his planet-destroying LEGO structure. Peace of mind.

We could believe it. We could easily believe that Wilt would hardly wear his leather slipper and that somehow the missing LEGO piece would suddenly appear in that sadly unused slipper. We believe wholeheartedly in the circle's, in the APP's, disbelief, in their shock. We only find it hard to believe that a grown man would find this eventuality so unbelievable, because we always overestimate the intelligence of the average human.

Man, I can't wait to fit this piece into the Death Star, Wilt said.

The Death Star rules, Dim said.

What's a Death Star?

Star Wars, Ricky, Dim said. The machine of the Dark Side.

Dark Star, no one said.

It's pretty frickin' cool, Mr. Ridicoloso said.

Wilt was nodding.

You bet. You bet it is.

Wilt or Dim could've said this, but since the phrase was repeated, we're betting hard unConfederate money that it had been Dim.

I'm not going to deny that having a machine of the Dark Side — as Dim puts it — with the capability of exploding planets is supercool, Peeps the Frogman of Doom said. But is it a little weird that you're still playing with LEGOs?

Sharp intakes.

I mean to say, that you're maybe a little too old for Star Wars, I suppose.

Head shakes.

I mean, it's not bad, I'm not saying that it's bad. It's just maybe a bit juvenile, maybe, for an adult who's trying to start a new political party, I suppose, to be building Death Stars out of LEGOs, I guess, and to have lost one of the pieces, too.

Fingers not stuffed into jeans out wagging.

I mean to say . . .

Peeps looked down.

I guess I should shut the heck up.

Ricky shrugged.

Maybe Star Wars is a bit silly, he said.

Sharp intakes, head shakes, wagging fingers.

We got way off topic, Wilt said. There's absolutely nothing silly about Star Wars or adults being into it or into building LEGOs or especially in building LEGO Death Stars.

Death Stars are pretty awesome, Mr. Ridicoloso said.

There are more than one? Ricky asked.

Return of the Jedi, Dim said. In Jedi there's another Death Star.

Almost, Peeps said. It was under construction and then it was blown up.

Blow up the planet exploder? Ricky said with very real, very bony confusion.

Whoa. Peeps put up his hands. That's actually kind of deep, Ricky.

Ricky Limes smiled.

Let's get this back on the Appropriated Patriot Party, shall we?

Wilt placed the once-was-lost-but-now-is-found LEGO piece on the mantle beside the gun and the COVID Christmas portrait and vintage cookbooks and porcelain knickknacks.

You're right, Dim said.

Sorry, Mr. Ridicoloso said.

Of course, Peeps said.

Sí, sí.

Ricky kept on grinning.

Where we go one, we go all.

Where we go one, we go all, the rest chorused.

So we all know how the libtards are strangling America with their participation trophies and hoppy beer and bespoke soap and gender confusion and who knows what, Wilt said. And libtards are snowflakes and everyone knows how snowflakes melt when there's heat, and I say we apply some darn heat and make some libtard soup.

Wilt smiled at his own cleverness. If there had been a reaction button in the Corley's wide living room, he would've hit that dang thing with a hugged heart.

Libtard soup, Dim said. Good one.

Wilt Corley kept his mouth open:

WHY THE PATRIOT PARTY IS SO FREAKING AWESOME

America's been knocked off its axis, even if it's really flat and not a ball like a blue and green marble hanging in space, if we were to take what the scientists say at their word, which I don't. America, I say, has been knocked off course and we need to dig a better path toward . . .

We're stepping in a moment to let you know that this just goes on and on. Wilt mentions how the COVID vaccines make you magnetic and infertile and are used as governmental tracking devices and peeking behind the curtain and red and blue pills and a one world government and death cults with poison jabs and dudes getting married and millennials getting it too darn easy and rampant wokeness ruining Marvel movies and rigged elections and the revision of history and face masks God what's with all the face masks and the Russians are coming the Russians are here the Russians stole the election with the Dominion machines and how they're the real Death Stars and oh oh oh have you heard they're putting the COVID vaccine in salad dressing?

This was some of it, not all of it, and we thought it best to trim the list to the least crazy shit. Seriously. It gets worse.

Did you say flat earth?

Peeps the Frogman of Doom scratched his full head of hair and failed to dislodge an explanation.

Wilt looked as serious as a heart attack, which, to be fair, he most probably was brushing up against at that exact moment, braced against the mantle and swaying. One of his knees popped when he shifted legs to say:

Do your research. It's all there. I've got sites I can send you showing how the earth is flat as a disc golf disc.

Bro, Dim said. How do you explain that while we are heading from spring to summer, Australians are heading from fall into winter? Love and respect, man, but you are way off on this.

Unmasked. Unmuzzled. Unvaccinated. Unafraid.

We guess.

General Confusion had been the one to tell Wilt about the COVID vaccine in the salad dressing. He had been a general, right?

We know, we know.

False information. Checked by independent fact-checkers. Partly false information. Checked in another post by independent fact-checkers. Fact check about a Hermann Göring quote that's meant to scare people into believing lies. Flagged in social media's ongoing efforts to seem like they give a shit without picking a side. See why. See photo. Visit the COVID-19 Information Center. Grab a pamphlet. Get a jab. Get vaccine info. I am the way, the truth, and the life. Mainstream media mainlining designer drugs designed for gay dogs in feather boas. Transhumanism has started. Bitcoin mining. Get vaccine info. You've got your pamphlet, right? We've all been duped by Dr. Fauci. Save America. The Nuremberg Code. Visit the COVID-19 center. Did you throw your pamphlet away? Did you throw it in the fire along with your lithium batteries? Elon Musk ox. Bitcoin crashing. Blue Origin rising. Truth seekers. Trust us trust us trust us. Sheeple. Herd immunity. NGOs. Get vaccine info. Jesus, why'd we even give you a motherfucking pamphlet? Trust the science. Deny the evidence. Pharma propaganda. Censorship. A ship of fools, stuffed with incense, lit on fire. Foolish ships fashioned from gopher wood, holy spit, and indignation. The word of God. Follow the science, follow the lie. Cabal puppet. Kissing the hands of Rockefeller and Rothschild. Shut down social media for thirty days. Irony. Church of Satan. May be an image of one or more people. Praise you for all you do. Twitter for Android. Paranoid or otherwise. In the know. Altered video. The same altered video was checked by the fact-checkers. Independent checkers. Political affiliation. See why. See video. Related videos. CLAIM. media.tghn.org. They're experimenting on Americans. COVID-19 vaccines go through many tests for safety. For effectiveness. Monitored closely. Get vaccine info. Don't eat the salad dressing. Fuck your pamphlet.

Wilt's mouth was always open:

Well, Dim, the sun moves North and South of the equator during its orbit, and also higher and lower in the firmament creating the seasons.

DISCLAIMER.

Wow, Peeps the Frogman of Doom said. Just, wow.

I couldn't have said it better, Dim said, if it were a thing I would've said.

(He's already said this. We've told you. Remember?)

Do we still get a gun?

Ricky was smiling without a hint of confusion.

I'm still confused, I guess, Mr. Ridicoloso said, what this has got to do with the Patriot Party.

The Appropriated Patriot Party, Dim said. Sheesh. We've already named it.

One could almost say that the name's been stolen, Peeps muttered.

Wilt slapped the mantle.

Man, would you stop being so negative, Peeps? And quit your muttering, while you're at it. Passive aggressiveness, passive aggression, the passion and anger, whatever, is not cute and it's not funny and it ain't helping a thing right now.

Dim obliquely eyed Peeps.

Yeah, Dim said. Wilt's right on that one, Peeps. You're either with us or you're against us. And if you're against us, then you've lost 'cause there's no way we're going down without a fight.

Where we go one, we go all, Peeps said. I get it, I get. I'm with you guys, I swear. You know me. Cut me and I bleed red.

To be fair, though, Mr. Ridicoloso said. I do have some gay friends and, quite frankly, I don't care if they want to be married or not.

Bro, Dim said.

Guys kissing guys? No, no, no. That's no bueno.

I mean, Peeps piped in, the very idea grosses me out, but if dudes want to get it on then . . .

Peeps shrugged and there was nothing of doom in the shrug. He'd trample people on the way out of a burning building.

Of course, we're speculating. Can you blame us?

Guys, guys, Wilt said, arms out as wide as he could stretch them, which was far less of a span than his big screen TV, let alone the living room wall, but greater a span than his arrhythmically beating heart.

Late nights with video games, poor diet, lack of exercise. We're waiting for his heart to storm the Capitol.

Tap tap tap tap.

Lucky!

God, guys. It's Lockheed. Get it straight.

What's he got in his mouth now?

Wait.

Wilt's heart dropped into his stomach.

The headset to a Vive Cosmos Elite. Lockheed had the band between his jaws and, dipping his head when he saw his owner glowering at him, let the front cover over the lenses bang on the bamboo floor.

Wilt moved as quickly as Wilt could move and went to a knee with a pop and groan.

Lockheed, Lockheed, he said. Bad boy, bad bad boy.

Lockheed whimpered and lowered his head some more and ground the cover into the floor.

Give it up, Lockheed. Give it up, boy.

It's got the cover on, Dim said. It should be okay.

Come on, boy.

Wilt was able to get the dog to release the headset. He patted Lockheed's head. Lockheed whimpered some more, turned, and skulked off like a chastised missile.

Wilt stood up.

Do you know how much these things cost?

He held out the headset for all to see.

A million córdobas?

What? No, Ricky. I'd assume it's far less than that.

I assume the question's rhetorical, Dim said.

Wilt shook his head and gently placed the headset on the mantle beside the LEGO piece, the gun, the COVID Christmas portrait, the porcelain knickknacks, and the vintage cookbooks God cook the books God just make sure the books are about cooking goat and not sheep since eating the flesh of the sinners is okay according to Jehovah War Theory or maybe someone else's god.

A lot, guys, Wilt said. It costs a crap load of money. Top of the line gear, there. It isn't some second-rate Oculus that just anyone can buy.

I've got an Oculus, Mr. Ridicoloso said. Works great.

Yeah, well, how'd you feel if your dog came into the living room with it banging on the floor?

Mr. Ridicoloso considered the floor.

Not very good, he muttered.

I'm not even sure how he got the thing off the stand without knocking it over. Wilt scratched his chest. I mean, we would've heard the sound, right? The thing falling?

Well, Peeps the Frogman of Doom said with his arms out, how did he get the gun out of its case?

What case? A gun case for my handgun? What are we, Democrats?

Heck no, Dim said.

No way, Mr. Ridicoloso followed.

Liberals try to ruin my country.

That's right, Ricky. Wilt nodded. The liberals ruin everything. Even your homeland. Poor, poor Argentina.

Nicaragua.

Whatever.

Wilt tapped the side of the headset.

This is the only mask you'll ever catch me wearing, he said.

Amen.

Agree to disagree, Peeps said.

How's that?

Batman's mask is pretty cool.

Peeps popped his teeth in a grin.

Wilt pointed a trigger finger at him and depressed that trigger, shaking his head, while everyone laughed and laughed.

But, seriously, Mr. Ridicoloso said. Maybe we shouldn't judge people for wearing a mask. He shrugged. It's their choice, their body. If they want to cover up their face, I say let them.

That's not the point, Wilt said.

Then what's the point?

That the government is lying to us, Wilt pressed on. That the CDC is a puppet of the Deep State, changing their narrative to suit whatever's convenient to them. The turth is out there, though, and the turth will out.

Did you say turth?

No, I said truth.

You said turth.

Turth doesn't even make sense.

That's why I asked.

Wilt smiled through annoyance at Peeps.

Well, anyway, if you misheard me, I meant it to be clear that I was talking about truth. And the truth will out.

Amen, someone said.

It still doesn't matter who'd said it.

From what you see in the news, Wilt charged on, you'd think the Conservatives are causing all the problems, or the Republicans, however they're framing it, when we all know it's really Black Lives Matter and Antifa and the Dems that are stroking discontent. Stirring and stirring the poop-pot and thinking that the rest of us aren't aware, that we're not watching at all.

Wilt leaned in toward the center of the circle.

But we are. We're always watching and always waiting and always ready.

Amen, someone said.

It still doesn't matter who'd said it.

I mean, there's a Q and there are As. Wilt patted the soft spot over his heart. Q puts out coded posts and the Anons are independent critical thinkers who decipher the Q posts and connect the dots. Q and all the anonymous truth seekers know that there is an information war going on right now and that they are the soldiers out there fighting it, fighting for freedom across the world.

Was Wilt Corley tearing up?

We don't even care anymore.

He opened his mouth since it was impossible for him to shut it:

Seventeen aka Q is the one that has the Cabal running scared, we all know it. Wilt pushed away from the mantle to lean in further. The real question is, who is Q, anyway? JFK, Jr., maybe? Hmmm? Hmmm?

Uh . . . Peeps held up his finger. JFK, Jr. went down in a plane.

Wilt dared to lean in further.

But did he die?

Yes, Peeps said. Yes, he died. Kind of hard not to in a plane crash.

But where's the proof, huh?

There were two others on the plane, too. The bodies were recovered. There was debris in the ocean.

I ask again. Wilt was about to topple over. Where's the proof?

I mean . . . Peeps scratched at an eyelid. There were autopsies performed. They died upon impact. They were cremated. Everyone knows this.

Wilt leaned in so far now his knee popped.

Were they? Were they, though?

There's a Wikipedia page on it. Peeps held his eyelid closed so it wouldn't flutter. You can check it.

Wilt Corley laughed and straightened up in his wide-oh-so-wide living room. His reflection in the eighty-five-inch TV laughed along with him.

Fitting symmetry, that, for Wilt Corley was the kind of guy who 'likes' his own posts. We have this on good authority. Believe us. We've seen the bodies and the debris. There was a memorial service. The cremated remains were scattered in the Atlantic. Sometimes Wilt was the only one to react to his own posts.

Just like Wikipedia's got a page on Antarctica, he said, even though it doesn't exist.

Come again?

Someone had said it and we really, truly don't give a flying squirrel turth who did.

There is no continent of Antarctica, Wilt said. If there was, then why aren't there any photos from 'space' of it. Hmmm? Hmmm? We've been indoctrinated to believe a Satanic lie.

Uh . . .

Ribs and brisket, round two. Here it comes. Wilt's already given the post a thumbs up. We're ready. Are you?

In reading Proverbs 17 this morning, Wilt continued, I came across an interesting passage: 'Sensible people keep their eyes glued on wisdom, but a fool's eyes wander to the ends of the earth.' That's Proverbs 17:24 of the New Living Translation. When seeking wisdom concerning all who declare the glory of God's creation and who discern Satan's deceptive twisting of turth . . . well, I have a question.

It's truth, dang it, Peeps said. Truth.

We don't think Wilt Corley even heard him. He just went on and on and on:

Where does the earth end, or does it? What are the 'ends of the earth'? The end of the known world, of civilization, or is there even a real actual end to it? Could the Ice Wall be the end of the earth the Bible is referring to? What is beyond it, or is it all just a foolish distraction? Because 'ends of the earth' is written at least twenty-five times in the Bible. There's so much we don't know about creation and so much that's viewed through a non-creator lens that we are taught to see with from birth. We are all beautifully and wonderfully made by intelligent design, by a benevolent Creator, God Almighty, creator of heaven and earth, and he extends, he only, to the ends of the earth.

A man said this. An actual man. A real and actual man designed by intelligence that wasn't all that intelligent, apparently, or else he or she or it would've set this poor beggar straight. But we're not doing it. Not anymore.

Anyone who thinks otherwise, Wilt never tired of going on, is just trying to California my Texas.

Don't California my Texas!

Amen.

A man said this.

Wilt Corley pounded the mantle and the gun fell with a bang to the floor. It hadn't gone off, though it was loaded. Wilt popped and groaned his way to the floor.

Thank God it wasn't the headset, Wilt said, still kneeling. Those puppies ain't cheap.

A million córdobas, Ricky said.

He hadn't really said this. We only said that he did, choosing that country's currency as an amusing detail, because we believe him when he said that he's from Nicaragua. He could just as well be from Guatemala or Colombia or the fiery toe at the end of Argentina for all the Appropriated Patriot Party cared. He probably spoke better English than Wilt Corley did. His grammar and spelling were certainly better. He was very possibly a hell of a guy, wide-smiling, tooling around on a Harley and in far better physical shape than any other member of the APP, certainly far better than Wilt Corley with the king-sized chest, who right now, was struggling to stand with the gun in his hand.

What, exactly, would Wilt Corley think, an Anon amongst a sea of Anons, of this story that we'd written him into?

Maybe he'd pray for us. Maybe he'd laugh with his reflection. Maybe he'd shake his head and denounce us as the sheeple he'd always believed us to be, or worse, Satan's minions. Maybe he'd unfriend us and leave us to our own echo chambers. Maybe he'd invite us to the third round of ribs and brisket and beam and beam about how big his grill is.

What if we're vegetarians?

So was Hitler.

Christ, Godwin's Law.

We're fearfully and wonderfully made. Wilt Corley is fearfully and wonderfully made. Those who disagree with Wilt Corley are also fearfully and wonderfully made.

We shudder.

We don't waste time on prayer for him.

We dive to reclaim the wreckage, the bodies. We've fired up the crematorium, all while fires rage on the ice fields of Antarctica.

WHY THE PATRIOT PARTY IS SO FREAKING AWESOME

You can see them from space. They disappear in an arc. That green and blue object is in fact a globe and not a slice of deep-dish pizza, and that's where we'll end the food analogies since we can see drool collecting in the wet pink arcs of Wilt Corley's lips.

We'll let Wilt run the optics. We're tired of his irresponsible bullshit. Let him visit the COVID-19 Information Center on his own. Let him watch the video. Let him stumble his way toward the truth with his VR goggles. Let him load the bullets in his own gun. He can snap that final LEGO piece into the Death Star and hopefully it won't mean the death of our planet.

To the ends of the earth.

Or, maybe, with a little help from his friends in the Appropriated Patriot Party, he'll continue to make his castle of cherry-picked bricks and shit ever more unassailable. Who'd want to storm it, anyway? What would you get? A COVID Christmas sweatshirt? Maybe COVID itself? Death? A dog? A Death Star? The truth, the turth, the thrust, the trust, the mistrust, the misfiring gun, a blown-out kneecap?

For where we go one, we go all.

And we all fall down together.

A is for awesome.

Amen.

And a-fucking-women.

WHY THE PATRIOT PARTY IS SO FREAKING AWESOME

WHAT BECAME OUR GREATER PURPOSE

Long after their ears stopped popping, Ann turned to Alan on the plane and asked:

"You ready?"

He shrugged in his seat. "As ready as I'll ever be."

"I'll go first."

"My belly feels a little queasy."

Ann nodded. "I've read that the pressurized cabin can make you want to poop."

"Lovely."

"But it's most likely just the pressure." Ann's forehead wrinkled. "It is just the pressure, right? You don't actually have to go to the bathroom?"

"I highly doubt there's a bath in there."

"Stop being a smartass, or I'll call the whole thing off."

Alan shrugged again. "It was your idea in the first place."

"Yeah, but it was your idea to go on this trip. All the way to Bora Bora."

She nodded her head to the right. Alan had no idea if this were the direction in which their travel destination lay. Neither did she. It was a good bet, in fact, that no one on the plane even knew in which direction Bora Bora was nestled, if they were even bound for Bora Bora, instead stopping stone-deaf in Tahiti after their ears popped again.

"Fine," he said. "But I suggested it for the both of us."

He rubbed his belly.

"Are you sure you don't have to go?"

"Yes, yes. I'm sure."

"Because if you do, there's no way I can go through with it."

"I said I don't have to." He squirmed in this seat. "It's just the pressure."

She eyed him closely. His eyes didn't waver. She nodded and turned away. Alan exhaled and sank deeper into the foam rubber cushions.

Ann was looking around her, as if there were watchers noting her every move, ready to clamber over the seats after her and jabber in French or Polynesian even though it was far more likely that any gibberish aimed in her direction would be in English. American English gibberish.

Alan spoke American English gibberish fluently.

"God, I could go for some pork," he said. "You think they roast pork in Bora Bora?"

"You mean roast pigs?"

"Mmm . . . baby suckling pig."

Ann shook her head, and the invisible watchers had no idea at what she was shaking.

"Can we get this back on topic?"

"Yes, yes. Absolutely."

But Alan was still looking as if one of those watchers were petting the pink scalp of a baby pig in the middle distance. Nice little piggy wiggy.

A.E. Gibberish.

Magnate of American dissatisfaction. Purveyor of matrimonial ennui. Global telecommunications giant and that giant was blasting over and over how desperately many marriages, such as Ann and Alan's here, needed an injection of spontaneity, of excitement, of honest, blue-collared endeavor to make this marriage — any marriage, all marriages — more than merely the sum of its humdrum, American-made parts.

Like having a good ole fashioned fuck in an airline restroom.

"Say what?"

"I didn't say anything."

"You said piggy wiggy."

"I did?"

"Uh huh."

"Wow."

"So?"

Alan shook his head and erased everything in the middle distance with that motion.

"Let's roll."

Ann shook her head because if she didn't, she was totally going to tsk-tsk-tsk.

"On a plane, Alan? Really?"

"Oh, yeah, right." He fidgeted but that plastic-wrapped cushion wasn't giving. "Let's get it on."

"Okay, Marvin Gaye." Ann cracked her neck without there actually being a crack. "I'm not so sure I can go through with this."

"What? What? It was your idea."

"I know, Alan. You've already said that."

Alan opened his mouth to say something, but since this was a very rare moment in which he was conscious of his mouth being full of only American English gibberish and teeth, he shut his mouth and waited for his wife's annoyance to subside.

On a plane, nothing subsides. It dissipates. Or, like the unholy union of human waste and SkyKem, it freezes at high altitudes and slips out a plane's undercarriage to rain down on the masses or the spaces between those masses as blue ice.

"I'll go first," Ann said.

She was resolved. Her resolution was far stronger than Alan's misgivings. It was far, far stronger than their limply flagging marriage.

Blue ice falling from the sky.

Ann patted the armrests.

"All right. Give me about a minute before you head in."

Alan could've been sweating in the climate control and contributing to the freshly forming blue ice.

"I'm going to bang your brains out," he said.

Alan gulped. He sweated and fidgeted. He didn't look Ann in the eyes.

"All right, prince of soul," Ann said. "I'll meet you in the restroom."

Alan winked but it looked more like ptosis, and since Alan had no idea what that word meant, the invisible watchers whispered in his ear: pathologic drooping eyelid.

Ann stood up and shuffled past Alan in his seat. He watched her walk down the aisle, occasionally placing her hand to a head rest to steady herself and apologizing to complete strangers.

She eventually disappeared. Dissipated. Became an ice block.

Alan wiped blue crystals from his eyes.

He tried counting out a minute but stopped at fifteen since it seemed silly to count any further.

Piggy wiggy, piggy wiggy. I'm gonna crush you in the restroom. I'm the motherfucking Bonecrusher. The prince of Motown. Bone ya in the boneyard and make ya scream for more and all those screams get sucked down by the vacuum toilet that's faster than a Formula 1 car. Can you handle it?

At least this is what the watcher who'd crawled over toward Alan had rasped into his ear.

Blue Ice Ice Baby, Bonecrusher, A.E. Gibberish. The benefactors of American ingenuity, sticktoitiveness, and firm-footed gumption.

God bless America and Air Tahiti.

Had it been a minute?

Fifty-eight, fifty-nine, sixty, sixty-one. For good measure.

Alan had remembered to count after all. Or maybe a watcher had pointed at a wristwatch and Alan resumed somewhere far past fifteen.

Alan patted his own armrests but failed to stand up.

"Oh God, my belly is a little off," he said, though there was no one there to hear. No one visible, that is.

"Come on, old man." He made little fists. "It's for the wife. It's for us. For the marriage." He stood and his legs didn't shake. "I'm gonna bang the living crap out of you."

Maybe Alan almost believed it.

Alan believed he could throw up. Or shit his pants. God, can't the plane just go down instead?

If Alan were a needle, he would've threaded his way between empty and filled seats and jabbed the point to the restroom door and sewn himself in good and tight. But since Alan was a human, and not the bravest example of that flightless race, he made his way along the aisle like a poorly folded paper airplane does: aimless, unpredictable, and falling far short of its goal.

"Those are nice shoes," he said to someone as he nearly crashed into the side of their seat.

Since Alan had a mask on, and for all the pressure in the cabin in which he could barely stand, his speech sounded more as if he'd coughed into a pillow.

More American English gibberish.

That airline patron never knew how admired their shoes were.

Alan lightly pushed himself away. Somebody had kicked that sad paper plane toward the end where the restroom door sat with an occupied red rectangle above the stainless-steel handle. He knocked lightly and coughed. Nothing. He knocked louder and straightened his face mask. He looked around him. No one was watching. Not even the watchers.

The door breached. Ann whispered. Alan couldn't hear her and said so. Her hand came out with her arm and her back muscles yanked him through a crack just wide enough for a pot-bellied piglet to fit through. Or one masked and full-grown adult male human. Gurgling belly and all.

"What the hell?" he said once inside.

The door slammed shut. Ann locked it. She looked crestfallen. She wasn't wearing her mask but reached for it to put it back on.

"What gives?" Alan removed his mask. "And what the hell's that smell?"

Ann had her eyes closed. She opened them now and pointed behind her since she still faced the door, not even turning to look at Alan.

"We can't do it," she said.

"What the heck are you talking about?"

But then he saw it. A plump turd sitting heavy in the bowl. Heavy since Alan instantly depressed the flusher, was deafened by the crack in time and space, and watched in stunned wonder as the fat turd sat unmoved by the vacuum and jetting blue SkyKem, taunting the void where the trap door at the bottom once had been.

Dearly departed, we come here before this black hole to pay honor to the last great excremental testament to A.E. Gibberish's greatness. He'd eaten a whole island-full of pork the night before and chased it down with glass after glass of Tahitian Vanilla Punch. He'd gotten in a verbal altercation with an old man from Long Island who said he still could whip ole A.E. any day, anytime, anywhere. And that anywhere happened to be there and that anywhen happened to be just then.

No one knows what exactly ole A.E. had said to precipitate this septuagenarian's promise of violence, but since A.E. felt a grand ole gurgle in the ole Gibberish guts, he thought it best to turn the tide and buy the man—and the whole bar, in fact—round after round of Tahitian Vanilla Punches. The man said he drank bourbon, good ole American bourbon, so A.E. said of course and complied with the pugilistic codger's wishes. He then quickly excused himself, sat on the hotel restroom's toilet, surrounded by bamboo plants and imitation palm fronds, and farted louder than the ceiling fan until he finally gave up and returned to his plates of pork and glasses of Tahitian Vanilla Punch. He did indulge in one glass of Buffalo Trace, or whatever, to satisfy that ole timer with the skinny and ever-ready fists, and felt that he had swallowed, gestated, and was bursting at giving birth to a baby buffalo himself.

Alas, poor A.E. Boy, he'd have to carry that weight, carry that weight a long time. Until the next morning, in fact. On the plane, snugly hunkered into his first-class seat, when the bomb went off. He'd launched his way back to Economy and unloaded this turgid stillbirth in the toilet bowl and that burnt umber of a stillbirth stared back when he stood back up. Good ole A.E. had flushed, and flushed again, trying to shoo the turd into the yawning unknown with fanning fingers and fevered resolution. Alas, alas, the sadly departed wasn't going anywhere, not sliding gently into that good night, rageless and clinging to an existence that was never worth living. A.E. bolted from the restroom in horror and returned to his first-class seat damp with sweat.

You'll be missed.

But not now when Alan considered this prodigious, unshakeable bulk. His gears were turning in his head and Ann watched them spin their spokes and not disturb a molecule.

She shook her head, wagging a finger. "No, no, no, Alan. No way. We're getting out of here."

"But we've come all this way."

"I can't, I'm sorry." She stood up straight. "No, wait. Hold on, Alan. I'm not sorry. There's no way in hell we're having sex with that in the toilet."

She pointed toward the toilet. Alan didn't need to turn around. The impression of that monstrous turd stuck to the inside of his skull.

"If we keep flushing," he said, "the blue stuff kind of kills the smell."

Ann folded her arms. "What, you're going to flush between thrusts?"

Alan folded his arms, too. "If I have to. If that's what it takes to save our marriage."

"Save our marriage? Are you fucking kidding me?"

Alan darted toward the flusher and pressed it, smiling.

"See? You can hardly smell it now."

The blue chemicals splashed the turd from all sides, but they may as well have been waves hitting a concrete jetty.

"No way, no way." Ann waved her hands, mask still on. "There's no way we're screwing in here."

Alan shrugged. "You can keep your mask on."

The bottom of the toilet snapped back into place. The turd hadn't moved a micron, hadn't moved a muscle. It seemed large enough to actually have muscles.

"I can still see it." She slitted her eyes. "God, even from here."

"I'll stand in front of it. Block its view."

Alan made himself appear as large as possible, like prey when threatened by a predator, like a coyote or cheetah or whatever they've got as apex predators on Bora Bora.

It didn't work. He wasn't big enough to block the memory of the brown bulk cemented to the inside of the bowl.

Ann shook her head.

Alan flushed again to help with the smell.

"Jesus," Ann said. "They're going to think we've got some serious intestinal problem in here. Or Ebola."

"Who?"

"The attendants." Ann looked over her shoulders, both ways, even though there was nothing except the gray walls. "The passengers."

"The watchers," Alan said.

"The who?"

"Skip it."

Ann slumped her shoulders. "Good. There's no way I could go through with it."

"No, I don't mean skip the sex." Alan flushed again. "I meant that no one's watching us. No one cares."

"Would you stop flushing the damn toilet?"

"Just trying to help."

"You can help by following me out of here in exactly thirty seconds."

"Thirty?"

"Sixty, then."

"You're giving up?"

Alan flushed again.

"Yes, Alan." Hands up. "I surrender. The turd wins. You can stay here and jerk off if you must."

"Now, now, this was your idea."

Fire returned to Ann's eyes. Fire in the restroom. On a plane. With a giant turd. Not her husband, though Ann felt he was truly more than useless now. The inability of that great lump in choking its way down the hole, to fail at even nudging itself toward the opening, just sitting and soaking up climate control as if it were birthed for that express purpose—somehow, that turd wasn't the most repugnant thing in the room.

"If you say it was my idea one more time, Alan, I swear . . ."

She left the rest of that statement to fall flat and wet beside the turd in the bowl. Something ought to enjoy their company in this confinement.

Alan was smirking. "You going to push me out the plane?"

The last thing Ann wanted to see, besides that gigantic shit, was Alan's stupid twist of his lips like two worms duking it out for sole rights over that grand buffet in the bowl.

"I'm kidding, I'm kidding," he said, hands up.

"This isn't funny."

Ann's own smirk formed and belied her own statement. Eh, she was masked, anyway, and, well, screw it, what could they possibly do?

"Well, what the hell are we going to do about this?"

Ann said this meaning, 'what the hell else can we do except laugh at this ridiculous situation?,' not, 'what other sexual act would be quick and appropriate enough for this situation?' which is precisely how Alan took it.

"I've got an idea," Alan said.

"Oh God."

Alan unbuckled his pants and dropped his jeans and briefs to the restroom floor.

"Holy living fuck."

Though Ann was still smirking, she somehow managed to mix in a healthy dollop of disgust. Maybe it was the mask. Who can tell if a person's really smirking when wearing a mask, especially when that observer is a pantless and senseless baboon?

Alan was at half-mast.

"How in the world can you not be as flaccid as a gorilla right now?" she said.

"I don't even know what that means."

To be fair, Ann didn't either. She did believe that Alan was surely more simian than anything beyond homo erectus.

With pants around his ankles, he bent toward the flusher and hit the button again.

"Knock that shit off!"

Alan, naked thighs and naked eyes, stared at the bowl in wonder.

"It's not even moving. All that flushing, all that water, all that suction, and it just sits there."

"Alan, pull your pants up. It's time to go."

"I can't even smell it now."

Maybe he'd grown accustomed to the environment, like the one guy at his workplace who somehow could eat a sandwich on the bench before the lockers in the restroom, whether there's someone in stall number one or two or three dropping their own deuce on company time. Alan could almost go for a pork sandwich right now.

"How the hell can you think of food right now?"

"Oh, crap." Alan scratched at the belly above his bouncing penis. "Did I say that out loud?"

Ann slapped at his dick and connected with the head.

"Hey!"

"Pull your damn pants up."

"Come on, honey." Massaging his mistreated member. "It was . . . my idea to go on this trip, to try to spice things up a bit, and though it wasn't my idea to have sex in the airline stall, I'm game for it, still game for it, despite everything, if it means it'll make things the way it used to be between us."

He put his hand to her shoulder and she winced. "Don't make beg, baby. I'm a horrible beggar. Let's get this done."

Ann dropped her head. Her eyes refused to come to the bowl with the turd. Her eyes refused to sweep past that and look her husband square in the eyes. She refused to even see the walls of the plane and the sky screaming around those walls and the birds that could never keep up with the plane, jealous as jealous things can be when not graced a glimpse at this singular moment in their goose or hawk or eagle history (whichever bird can fly the highest).

"I can't."

Defeat somehow louder than disgust.

"How about this?" Alan took his hand and grabbed Ann's and led it to his penis, gun-shy and flush with expectation. "A quick hand job and it'll all be over."

Ann became brave and brought her eyes up to glare at Alan.

"Really?"

"Yeah."

"Like this?"

"Yeah, that's good."

"Not too dry?"

"There's soap."

Ann gave a few more pumps and then pushed Alan in the chest.

"You're a pig."

"What? I was nearly rounding the corner."

"You disgust me."

Alan grabbed at his stomach and gurgled loud enough to almost sound like he'd depressed the flusher again.

"Oh, God," he said. "I gotta crap."

Ann took off her mask to show her husband her face. It was a blackhole. It swallowed everything. The toilet with the monster turd, the restroom, the plane with all the passengers, the geese and hawks and eagles, the invisible watchers of human folly, the puffy clouds that could be used as toilet paper, the blueness of the sky itself that could never SkyKem all these planes full of all these humans with their bloated and unflushable endeavors who'd dared to dream of despoiling tropical islands with their gigantic American fundaments.

"Hooboy," Alan said, and sat his ass on the toilet.

Ann put on her mask and the blackhole outside of their universe resituated itself directly under Alan's naked ass.

"Give it sixty seconds," she said.

"Lord, I'll need more than that."

She dared one last glance and Alan's hand came up, like Han Solo's did in Empire before he was frozen in carbonite. But instead of a declaration of love, there was a declaration in his eyes and wrinkles of his face and the muscles spasming in the corners at his extreme need to defecate.

"Go!"

My love.

She went.

He went.

And they were never quite the same couple again.

Some would say that this trip to Bora Bora, after all, wasn't a complete loss.

That's something that Alan and Ann would have to discuss once their ears popped upon descent toward the airport in Tahiti.

God's great urge.

A.E. Gibberish in first class dreamed of piggy wiggies on plates and tall glasses of rum mixed with exotic fruits.

WHERE THE COOL KIDS GO IN NEW BRAXTON OR DOVERTON

They didn't know where they were going. They knew where they wanted to go, but they couldn't make the knowledge of where they wanted to be match with their reality. The environs were their reality, and that reality consisted of mostly paved streets. Some of these were brick-lined, but nevertheless, they totally knew where they wanted to go.

Where was that? Well, always and ever in the opposite direction in which they were perambulating.

Who were they?

He: Lewis.

She: Lauren.

They: the coolest kids within two hundred feet.

Like young couples do when they've got nothing else to do, they went in search of something that would justify their walk of non-intention. That may seem depressing, but since they both never considered what the concept of non-intention could be, they were perfectly at peace in trying to discover that something through nothing and more aimless nothing.

That sounds bleak, we know. It's not bleak. It's blissful. All while the sun shone like the sun does when not obscured by clouds or the memory of any Pink Floyd album.

Lewis had his right bicep wrapped in plastic since he'd recently received the thousand-and-one jabs of inked intention into his flesh. What was the tattoo? You'll have to ask Lewis. We've no idea what it represents. We're a different generation with a different lexicon and legend to unlock our own meanings. Our own set of rules never required that they be indelibly needle-pricked into skin.

Lauren was the frontwoman of a very intentional, very heavy, very brick-lined-throated hardcore band called Your Bitch Smells Like My Bitch. Lewis loved it. He loved her. And all was right whilst perambulating.

Or nearly.

They were indeed walking, but where they went kept ending. Not like the sidewalk in the children's book. It was more in the form of mature human design, not childish whimsy, that thwarted them. More on that later.

Lewis scratched at the bottom bit of the plastic wrap on his arm. He failed to hit the offending spot since that spot was fully encased in that thin, unbreathable sheet.

Lauren, well . . . she could write a song about the whole affair. Already did, in fact, and that song sounded exactly like the window AC unit they both passed in heading down Hazelnut Street toward the culmination of their original intention.

Which had been exactly nowhere.

Lauren's hair was aquamarine. It flowed off her shoulder like water in a painting.

Lauren spoke first:

—Where are we going again?

—Hell if I know.

—So, we just keep walking?

—I guess. Isn't that what we're doing?

—But, I mean, is there a point?

—Does there have to be?

That specter of a point died on the tarmac. They kept walking. They never acknowledged that death. That death never needed acknowledgement. Like when you squash a palmetto bug on brick. It crushes in a creamy pus and then you just walk on.

Such is existence.

A door opened. It was a door to a bar. A really old bar. That bar was somewhere off Vance or Cabic or Church alley. The smell of puke and stale cigarettes wafted out the space.

—Should we go in?

—If'n we go in we'll maybe regret it, but if'n we don't we may regret it more, but if'n we just stall like mules at the gaping hole afore us then we my as well be led along with a tether and saddled 'cause we're nothing better'n animals braying at the sun. Or moon or dirt or somepin defin'lly more substantial than the greenery outside the backyard porch. And then you're caught. Good and well caught in the shiny surfaced wall of regret that'll haunt you and your spouse and your chil'ren for life ever arter into a somepin that ain't a nothing arter all.

—Shiny-surfaced wall? You mean a window?

—A winda, yeah, kinda like.

Lauren shook her head of aquamarine ombré hair.

—Remember what I said? No Joad before dinner.

—Sorry, babe.

—Call me by my damn name.

—Yes, yes. Sorry.

Lewis looked at his feet.

—You folks coming in or you just going to stand there like stunned mules?

Lewis' mouth dropped open.

—No, we were just looking, Lauren said. Thank you.

She waved and looked to Lewis whose awe shifted into mild humor. They spun on their heels and kept on down Front Street.

So they knew where they were, just not where to they were ultimately headed.

—We have to get back home for your band practice.

—There's no band practice today.

—Was it cancelled?

—We never have band practice on Saturdays.

—You don't?

Lauren shook her head.

—So then, when do you guys get together?

Lewis scratched at his scalp. He had very short hair. What little there'd been was dyed cool silver.

—Sundays, Lauren said. It's always been Sundays.

—Huh.

They kept walking down the sidewalk on a decline toward an intersection. Lewis pulled up and looked at the blue street sign and scratched his scalp again.

—Wait. I thought we were on Front. When did the street change to Prospect?

—There is no Prospect Street in Doverton.

Lewis pointed at the sign.

—Huh, Lauren said. Maybe they changed the name.

—What? While we were walking?

Lauren shrugged. Her fuchsia hair waved around her.

Lewis blinked rapidly.

—Hold on. What the heck?

—Heck? What are you, six years old?

—Your hair.

Lewis was pointing at Lauren's head now.

—What about it?

—It was green before.

—Aquamarine.

—Yeah. Lewis nodded. Aquamarine. Your hair was aquamarine.

—My hair was aquamarine like a month ago.

—It was?

—It was.

Lewis put away his pointer finger. The streetlight changed. The walk signal came on. They headed across the street.

—Poor fella don't have no hands or feet and yet he keeps awalkin' and going nowhere, stuck on the left side like a bug on a screen door.

—Lewis—

—And maybe there's a kinda contentment to just bein' stuck in limbo and seein' the other side a where you wanna go and crook-backed just on humpin' over.

—Lewis!

Lewis started laughing.

—You're Joading again.

—Sorry, sorry.

Lewis kept laughing.

They made it to the other side and the street sign read Water. They weren't even striding along the river. Lewis hadn't noticed this. Lauren had.

—When did we hit Water Street?

—Water Street? We're on Front.

—You mean we were on Prospect.

—Oh, yeah. We're on Prospect.

—The sign we just passed said it was Water.

—It did?

—It did.

Lewis scratched his head while walking, abstracted like a man with no hands and feet.

—Don't go Joad on me now, Lauren said.

Lewis laughed because he nearly embarked on a fresh Joad jaunt and not only knew that Lauren had sensed it, but also knew that Lauren maybe knew him better than he'd thought she had.

There was never any mystery about Lewis for Lauren. Maybe that's what she liked about him. His predictability. Sometimes predictability is the kind of comfort, the kind of familiarity all humans crave.

Like streets retaining their names.

Like knowing where you're walking, even when you're not walking anywhere.

They passed a coffee shop. They didn't go in. They didn't look at their reflections in the plate glass. They looked straight ahead until they didn't. Well, Lewis at least had looked away.

—Okay, he said. Now I know someone's messing with me.

—What do you mean?

—That sign there says Fiske Avenue.

—And?

—Well, it's like the street names have switched from Doverton to the ones I grew up on in New Braxton.

—Whatevs. You got a hip flask I don't know about that you've been hitting?

Lewis stopped and put out his arms wide.

—There's no Fiske Avenue in Doverton.

—I know that, Lauren said.

—Then how do you explain that sign?

—I can't.

Lewis' mouth fell open again.

—And now your hair's purple.

—Purple?

—Yeah, purple.

—It's Electric Amethyst.

Lewis snorted, but even though Lauren knew what that snort would precipitate, she was powerless to stop what was coming.

—I don't care if it's Lectric Amathingy or lavender or purple damn dinosaur, it weren't that color afore and you knows it and yourn refusing to fess up to it to befuddle me for no good reason.

—Lewis.

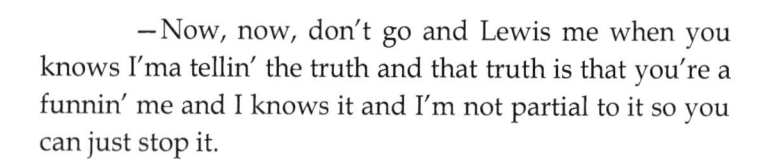

—Now, now, don't go and Lewis me when you knows I'ma tellin' the truth and that truth is that you're a funnin' me and I knows it and I'm not partial to it so you can just stop it.

—Lewis.

—Like the damn road names aroun' here switchin' and a swatchin' like a dern donkey's tail tryin' to get at the buzzin' flies hoverin' its backside.

—Well, that's usually where the tail is.

—Now, don't go and change the sub—

—Shut up with the Joad already. God.

Lauren cracked her neck with a full rotation of her head.

— I should've never let you read that book to me.

Lewis looked hurt.

—But I like to read to you.

—Put your damn arms down.

Lewis complied. He shrugged.

—Your hair wasn't purple, though.

—Electric Amethyst. And yes, it was.

—Fine. You win.

—And, that sign doesn't say Fiske. It says Market House Alley.

Lewis turned to the nearest street sign. It did indeed say Market House Alley.

—Does Doverton even have a Market House Alley?

—Well, dummy, you're staring at the sign, aren't you?

—I'm befuddled.

—Don't.

Lewis didn't. Instead, he shrugged again and said:

—Let's follow where it leads.

Lauren considered this for a second. Then for a second more. Eventually a flurry of seconds clumped together, but it was enough to make a full minute.

—Yeah, she said. I'm game.

They both went down the alley.

And what was at the end?

Another alley. Quince Alley, to be precise.

At the end of this alley?

Yet another alley. Muter Alley. Both had never heard of it.

At Muter's ending?

Another damn alley. Henderson Alley, this time.

And then what?

You guessed it. More alleys. Smith into Wilkinson into Wrights and that one dumped them onto Prince between Water and Front.

—There's the river, Lewis said, pointing.

—You're a genius.

—Thank you.

—How the hell did we end up here?

—We followed the alleys.

—Yeah, but how did they lead us here? To the river?

—Well, Lauren, I'd like to know how your hair went Emergency Cone Orange.

—It's Sunset Orange.

—Fine. But it's orange now and it was just purple.

—Just purple. You mean last week when it was Electric Amethyst?

—Jesus Christ, babe, you're getting me all tuned up and fit to Joad.

—Shut your face.

—I'ma shuttin' it.

At this point a beggar showed up, as if from air. Not thin air since it was summer and the atmosphere was far too three-tiered-cake thick to have anything spontaneously appear. Maybe a blob. A great fat gelatinous cube, perhaps, but not anything as solid as a beggar. He must've shambled into the frame while Lauren and Lewis weren't watching, while they were naming street signs and hair dyes.

    —Spare some change?

    —Uh, yeah, I'm sure I've got something.

Lewis patted down his tight khakis that were totally not stuffed with any legal tender: paper or coin. And certainly not a chicken with which to barter.

Spare some fowl?

    —Here's a dollar, Lauren said, handing over the bill.

The beggar's smile dropped. His face got dire. He clutched the bill to his chest and seemed about to embark on his own Tom Joad story.

    —No, no, no, Lauren said.

    —But, ma'am—

    —I've got nothing else. Seriously.

    —But the kids—

    —I gave you my only dollar.

—But surely, ma'am—

Lewis was still patting his thighs.

The beggar never finished his statement.

Lauren stared him down until he turned slowly on his heels and walked away, mumbling, Thank you, ma'am.

Lauren could stare down a cat. In fact, she did so once on the front porch in the early morning at a black and white feral cat that had stopped with one paw in the air and glared like only a cat can glare. Well, except for Lauren. She'd slowly backed herself into the wicker rocking chair, never breaking eye contact with the cat, and sat down and set herself to slowly rocking. The cat had put down its paw but didn't drop the stare. They both sat and stood there for at least ten minutes solid. Beggar solid.

(Maybe.)

Surely five minutes.

(Okay.)

If you've ever stared down a cat, then you know how long that takes.

We've never stared down a cat.

—Does that sign say Harrigan Lane? Lewis asked.

Lauren waited until the beggar skulked down an unmarked and unnamed alley. That's when she finally broke visual contact.

—There's no Harrigan Lane in Doverton, she said.

—Christ in a bucket of rusty nails, Lewis said without pointing. Now your hair's green.

—Emerald.

Lewis shrugged.

Time dilated. Streets and alleys combined, split apart, and recombined over distance. Straight lines became crooked. Crooked lines skewed ever more crooked. Egresses and ingresses met and kissed and flapped fleshy tongues in the middle of the intersections. The world wept to watch it, meaning that it started to faintly drizzle.

—Where to now?

Lauren had no answer since there never had been an answer to this question.

Where were they going?

—I guess that way's not so bad, she said.

Lauren threw her black-as-night tresses off her shoulders.

—Midnight Kiss, she said.

—What?

—Nothing.

They kept walking.

—What's the name of the alley that runs next to the house next to ours?

Lewis scratched at his silver head. The color of his hair had never changed.

—Crap, he said. You know, I don't rightly know. And that's a funny thing, like when you hit your dern funny bone and there's a nothin' funny about—

Lauren tripped Lewis on the sidewalk and he sprawled out as if he'd hit a patch of ice. She glared down at him with her blond tresses and Lewis wasn't even sure who he was looking at.

—What street are we on?

He'd said this after he'd said OW.

Lauren scanned the environs for street signs. She broke eye contact. Lewis swept his leg and hit air.

—Not this time, buddy.

—Crap, he said again.

Lewis laid his head on concrete. He looked up at the street sign in blue with the declaration of a Historic District above the white street letters.

—Noname Street? Is that Japanese? Lewis asked.

Lauren shook her head.

—I can't knock you down if you're already on the ground.

—When did you get band t-shirts made?

Lauren looked at her chest. So brave. Breaking eye contact again.

—Your Bitch Smells Like My Bitch has always had shirts.

—Why don't I have one?

Lauren blinked twice. Hard. You could almost hear the lids grind up and down.

—You have to be one of the cool kids, she said.

—Ah.

He didn't understand. Maybe Lewis never would. But in that moment . . . God, she was so goddamn hot.

WHERE THE COOL KIDS GO IN NEW BRAXTON OR DOVERTON

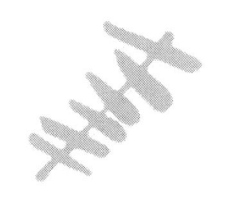

WHO COSGROVE SAW

Cosgrove was a man who wrote one-word poems.

People on the street came up to him and asked him to write them poetry, much like curbside painters will paint your portrait upon request — on the fly, on the cheap.

No one came up to Cosgrove for poetry.

That's a fib. A fib is a quaint word for a lie. A lie is the way in which a golf ball is situated on the course. The type of people who care about this specific definition of the word 'lie' are the type that Cosgrove would amble toward, hat in hand, to beg for money.

Yes, Cosgrove was a beggar.

He had a bevy of one-word poems at the ready, but he preferred spontaneity over structure, and so usually brandished a blank scrap of paper alongside the ballcap cupped in his left hand. The right, of course, gripped mightily his pen.

To be fair, though, Cosgrove hardly ever cared if he received money, though he was always nearly starving. He cared more for the written word, for his poetry. He had integrity baked to the brown skin of his forearms while he held out the hat.

Cosgrove was not a person of color.

He was a white man, though just barely, to the white people whizzing past him on the busy route toward the bridge to the next town.

He was a person of poetry. One-word poetry.

Once he'd written:

Knite.

Another time:

Lyfe.

Still another:

Cornmudgeon.

And once more:

Neptunalia.

The stores were endless. Much like his mind, they were always stuffed with gold-minted one-word poems. Forget the syllables. That never mattered.

Cosgrove once wrote a poem that went:

NevercaredtoaskyournameandnowIwishIhad.

Which was kind of cheating, even Cosgrove would admit, but he'd still shake his ballcap after handing over the dirty slip of paper with the poem on it and light — lighght — would glint in his eyes.

He'd open his mouth. He'd not get to say a word or even apply the tip of his pen to paper and push out inked inspiration in a sweaty stream. It was hot outside, and so he'd be shooed away to amble up and down the busy route along the median just before the bridge that led to the next town.

I don't have any money, he'd hear.

Or the light had just turned green.

Or simply a command to go away.

But where could Cosgrove go away to? Prepositions at the ends of sentences afforded far too little shade.

Cosgrove had once written:

Ammble.

Another time:

Hungr.

Once again, so succinctly it almost hurt his pride:

Hep.

These weren't cries for help as much as misunderstood missives at greatness. Great attempts. Big misses. Empty stomachs.

And so Cosgrove ambled.

It was so hot that the drivers in cars at the intersection without AC — windows rolled down, occupants visibly panting — were irritable at Cosgrove's approach. He'd only dare advance toward such vehicles under the greatest duress. He normally went for climate-controlled transport, since these seat-fillers were chilled, slightly guilty, still employed cash, and had an urgent need to scroll their driver's side windows back up once that guilt had been assuaged.

Up. Thank goodness that hadn't ended the previous sentence. Barely room for shade.

Cosgrove once made so bold to pen:

Ballsack.

Another time when it'd been particularly sticky out:

Vellcrow.

And still a third time in similar heat:

Meltingmeltinmelt.

Cosgrove shook his hat, and he had a quarter, several pennies, and a stone that someone thought hilarious enough to dump into his hat of poetry.

Hahah.

Above, another instance of Cosgrove's poetical genius. A palindrome, even.

Cars went by in a blur. Cosgrove himself was mostly a blur. Almost always. No matter how ready the pen, no matter how pitiable the hat, those cars and SUVs and motorcycles and scooters and bicycles just wheeled on by.

By. Shade. A perfume that Cosgrove would never wear.

Oh, the gems he'd unearth:

Tarmacintosh.

Or:

Ibeeunemployd.

Or:

Pelucidlea.

Well, that was poetry, indeed. Cosgrove knew that no one could truthfully deny him that.

I don't carry cash, someone had said.

Cosgrove wiped the sweat from his brow with the sleeve of his thin flannel shirt. He wore brand new sneakers, a brand that he'd never heard of.

Ov.

Above, another cogent poetical diamond. Heavy carbon compression.

Sometimes, a driver or passenger from a vehicle he'd approached would look down and make some snide remark about his glistening new sneakers. Cosgrove wouldn't look down, he wouldn't break eye contact, he was as guiltless as a cat. He could've told them that he'd gotten them free, a donation from a local clothing warehouse that sometimes dumped their unsellable returns into the hot moist cave of the Salvation Army truck.

Salve-ation.

This would be on the slip of paper he'd hand over to the person sneering at his sneakers.

Or maybe:

Armless.

Which wasn't a new word, but then poetry didn't always demand neologisms — even one-word poems.

Not everyone was condescending or callous to Cosgrove. Some were kind. Some helpful. Some even offered him a lift to that next town over the bridge in which he didn't live or, in fact, never been. Cosgrove never really cared to go. Those in the cars heading to the bridge to the next town were almost universally cold toward him.

Kindnestled.

Kindredspits.

Killsmeevreethyme.

That one was a bit of a stretch. Cosgrove knew this, but he was hungry, and hunger made him desperate. Desperation caused his pen to stumble, to fall into subpar poetical potholes. Misfires over the bow or over the water, it hardly mattered. When the deck or mast or even sail escaped harm, Cosgrove would sigh, his belly gurgle, and he'd move on.

On. To some shade, one would hope.

There was this one time, though, when Cosgrove saw someone that he knew. Or had known. This man in his sedan looked exactly like Cosgrove if Cosgrove had been given a fresh shave and haircut and a donation of new clothes to match his glistening shoes.

This man in the car, though, looked nothing like Cosgrove. Sometimes Cosgrove just let his mind drift, to inhabit the face of another human he'd envied from afar. It wasn't about the money. Not really. It was about respect. But then, respect could hardly buy one a sandwich. So, he'd take what he could get.

The man didn't have money in his hands. His fingers were gripped around the steering wheel.

Soffspot.

Weekness.

Dayafterdayafterdayafter.

The prepositional hangover couldn't jog Cosgrove's memory. He knew he knew this guy, though. And this guy stared back at Cosgrove as if he knew, too — the envied man — that Cosgrove knew that he knew him.

Newhim.

Creeturoflighght.

That last one Cosgrove had handed over to the man that he knew he knew. Cosgrove didn't break eye contact. No cats were underfoot or under tire. The man, however, let his shiny cool eyes drop to the slip of paper.

Cosgrove could feel the cold void emanating from the climate-controlled cabin. The man had been in an SUV, after all — not a sedan. Cosgrove shivered, and the shivering felt good, but he never broke the stare.

Okay, Sorokin, the man had said.

Cosgrove's heart sank. Right into his donated sneakers.

The man threw the slip of paper back at him, but since it hadn't been fashioned into a plane or dart or even a crushed ball, it caught the dead weight of the air and swished its way to the steaming tarmac.

Get a job, you bum, the man said, pointing.

Cosgrove didn't look behind him. He knew what was there: a gas station with a large white sign with red lettering declaring HELP WANTED.

A two-word poem. What extravagance. 'Help' would've been enough. Or 'Wanted,' even.

Or:

Hep.

(Again.)

Want.

(Simply that. The need.)

Thementalhealthofthegastationattendantisnotimportant.

Cosgrove afforded himself the luxury of a smirk. He hadn't broken eye contact. Not even now. Not even with the sweat in his eyes. He didn't stoop to retrieve the paper with the poem.

Heartlessness, he said.

He spoke a poem. And with that utterance, that singular judgement, he spun on the barely worn heels of his sneakers and strode on toward the next vehicle.

The light had changed before he got there.

The lighghghghghghghghght.

It was Saroyan, Cosgrove knew. Sorokin was a Russian writer, and everyone knows that Russian writers are crazy. They'd never be able to get a job at a gas station, no matter how badly the stations wanted the help.

Cosgrove would bet Sorokin stared down cats, too, if Cosgrove had any money to bet with.

With. Maybe enough shade after all.

Cosgrove would always write one-word poems., and though his belly would almost always grumble against the disdain or indifference of those in their cooled transports, he'd never ball his fist in anger.

Anger was poor fare, indeed. He'd rather eat his hat.

Cars were always driving along the main route that led to the bridge to that next town. Cosgrove would never make it over the bridge. The bridge was fashioned from the balled-up slips of paper with his one-word poetry. Year after year after year after.

Afterton. Maybe that was the name of that town. Cosgrove had never heard its real name, had never seen the sign that named it, had never believed that there even was a town over there. Maybe, too, the man in the SUV who'd seemed so familiar shared the name with the town. Cosgrove would hand that slip of paper with that invented name to the next person he'd approach. Then again, maybe he wouldn't.

He'd have to wait for the light to change, in any case.

Cosgrove had all kinds of time. His sneakers still had spring and squeak. His heart kept chugging poetry through his veins.

Chuggachugg.

WHOM WE MEANT TO KILL

We're part of the Bad Luck Club. We've got the bumper sticker. It's inches away from the crushed quarter panel. It's an inside joke. We know, we know. We see the irony.

As part of the assassination process, we make contact. We don't rely on middlemen. We're the beginning, the middle, and end of all men in our endeavor.

We're not all men, though, of course. We're equal opportunity. All are welcome within our organization of killers. It's only required we be adept, and not be bothered with an overgrown conscience.

Are you able?

So, this guy on our list, we gave him a ring. His name was Saben. We swear to God, that's his actual name. Someone picked up on the other end. We're not entirely convinced it was the Saben on our list. But then again, how many Sabens can there be?

Turns out, there are a crap ton of Sabens.

Well, we need to figure out which one's the right one so we can liquidate him. Or her. Could just be an avatar, for all we know. We need to know more.

Liquidate. Yes, we realize that's got a certain businesslike quality. We're in the business of murder, after all, and this dude Saben's going to die.

What did he do? We don't care. We don't ask. That's not our job, not what we investigate. We call, sure. We're not sloppy, we've got a reputation to maintain. We wouldn't want to jab the wrong fellow in the neck and drag him under a stairwell for him to good and comfortably bleed out his existence. We're professionals.

However, there are accidents, mistakes, no matter how methodical our approach. Some Sabens are going to fall through the cracks. We want to minimize the scrap rate, as it were, to sustain our viability into the foreseeable future. Automation won't come for us. If we're careful, and we're the very embodiment of carefulness.

It's our job to care.

There was this one guy, once . . . He wasn't named Saben. We think it was Steven? Or Kevin? Devin? Anyway, that poor sucker won't be a Steven or Kevin or Devin again.

Eh, you can't make a frittata without breaking some skulls.

Eggs are supposed to be symbolic of the soul. Whatever. Fragility. We get it. Life's always one second away from getting cracked or crushed. What good's a soul, then? Having a conscience is a liability to the life of an assassin. It'd be the death of us, for sure.

What else is new, though? The preacher said there wasn't anything new under the sun. We bet you've heard someone say that before.

Of course, that person was lying. There's always something new for finite beings. If you're a star, maybe, with a billion-year lifespan, everything will have been seen and done and repeated and witnessed anew until that witnessing itself becomes as insensate star dust.

But with sixty or seventy or eighty trips around a middling sun?

This guy Saben, the one we're looking for, has got far fewer years than that coming to him. If he were aware of us, which he's not, he'd surely make peace with his maker, or live life to the fullest extent allowed by our law, or gone all the way when it mattered instead of holding back, for we'll surely not hold back.

Maybe he'd hope in a chance for escape. A hope for clemency. Hope. It's a killer. It's worse than us. We're inevitability. Hope's the hand stretched to the billions-year-old star that burns the skin of that hand.

At least we make a phone call.

Saben? No? Saben? Not this one, either. Saben? Yes?

You're dead.

Your breaths have been numbered. We have an accountant who's ridiculously assiduous. She doesn't mind working overtime.

In time, we found our Saben. The correct Saben. The one we were meant to kill all along.

Are you Saben?

We'd asked, knowing full well that you were the Saben we'd been seeking. You'd be wasting the breaths left to you in speaking to us.

Yes? And you are?

So classic Saben, that. Of all targets, really. Not wanting to be impolite, but wary, nonetheless.

We've been looking for you.

We weren't playing. There's not time to be coy. We needed to judge your reactions. Often telling the truth straight out is the best option. People can tell a lie, even over the phone. But we were there in person, at your door, and we needed Saben, the correct Saben, to believe us.

Looking for me for what?

We needed to tantalize. A dash of mystery with the truth. The recipe for Saben's disaster would take time to prepare, getting the proper ingredients, slow cooking to perfection, plating the masterpiece with just the right amount of steam. Those bubbles under the dish slowly liquefying into a nice solid wedge.

You're a photographer, right?

Yes . . .

We understand it's awkward for us to reach you this way, out of the blue, but we've got a project, a special project, that demands a professional photographer, and you were the one recommended.

We?

Yes. The company.

Who are you?

We are the ones who were meant to find you, as we've said.

This may seem like we were too close to the edge. It's that hint of mystery, you understand. People want to believe. People want to believe that they can't be hoodwinked. People are firm believers in themselves, even when they've not got the experience or results to warrant that belief.

We've got all the faith in the world. We've got the training, put in the time. We've been playing with knives since we don't know when. We can't remember the number of throats we've slit. You'd have to ask our accountant, if she'd take your call.

Okay, this is getting weird.

We realize this is a bit unorthodox, Saben.

No, I mean, you guys need to tell me what this is all really about, who sent you, or I'm calling the police.

Yes, yes. We understand.

We dared place a hand to our heart. It wasn't a flat-out lie since we truly believed in our sincerity in killing you. We always took murder seriously.

We were sent by . . .

We said what we had to say to make you believe us. We lied a little. We mixed in more truth. You knew who we were speaking of, and you smiled at us. We smiled at you. We took you in. Over time, you opened the door and let us into your living room. You offered drinks. We accepted. You offered seating. We sat close to you where you sat in your soft brown club chair. You'd never heard of the Bad Luck Club and we'd never tell you. We all sipped and we all kept smiling.

So, then, what exactly is it I can help you with, in the way of photography?

During that spoken sentence, you hadn't noticed when we jabbed you in the leg with a pin, a tiny pin soaked with poison. You'd looked us in the eyes and then looked away to swat at a fly at your leg that had never been there. It'd been the unseen jab extracted.

You couldn't possibly know that you were already dead.

It's a matter of life and death, you could say, we'd said.

You seemed puzzled, but then you lolled in your chair. We could've caught you, but that's not why we were there. Since you were already dead, there was no reason to soften the impact with the floor. We were already headed to the door. We were out the door.

Damn fly, you'd said before we left.

We hadn't replied. We'd closed the door quietly. We'd walked away and towards our vehicle by the curb. The sun shone full on another domicile of a Saben who'd been the correct Saben, stretched out and stiffening on the floor.

We'd been paid before we'd arrived, so it was easy to forget you.

Just another liquidation. The balancing of the books. No one bothers over the life of a fly.

If we'd looked back, glancing over our shoulder upon exiting, would we have seen you in your own vomit, clutching at air, kicking at the seat cushion or legs of your comfy chair? Maybe. But we've seen it all before.

You were dead. That had been our job, you had been our job. No matter the particulars of the undoing, so long as you never breathed again, we could continue to hold faith in and be proud of ourselves for a job well done.

Those other Sabens, though. The ones who'd been killed.

Had there been others?

We're a big organization.

Cracks. Plans. Hopes. Existence.

For us it only mattered that you'd been the correct Saben for us, the one we'd been sent out to kill. Any others who may've been terminated were on someone else. We'd gotten paid. We'd done our duty. We'd even closed the door out of respect.

Respect for our profession.

What would've been better? To have snatched Saben, put a bag over his head, stuffed him into our SUV and driven him to an undisclosed location? We could've led him to the hooded behemoth in the basement. Introductions and nods. The executioner blinks, raises his double-headed axe, cuts off Saben's head and that head rolls to rest at a club chair's apron. Blink, blink, blink. All while the sun's outside and unaware.

We're not monsters.

We feel, however, impelled to tell the truth. We've been paid before for liquidating the incorrect person. Of course, we'd made it right by getting the correct target. But it's not unknown in our business to have collateral damage. Hell, nations do it all the time, and at a far higher rate. This isn't an excuse, you understand. That's why we do our research. For those rare times under the sun, though, where we make a mistake, we learn, we correct, we improve, we perfect.

And we always make it right.

Sabens are more prevalent than you'd think, though. We agree it's kind of a unique name, but then humans have a talent for theft, and stealing singular given names is no exception. We just happen to be the ones to snuff that or that or that iteration of whichever flame of Saben was meant to be snuffed.

The flame is a symbol of the soul, too, though we're not in the business of souls. We'll leave that to the priests and spiritualists.

So, this Saben, the correct Saben, is toast. He's part of the vomit in the carpet. The cleaners of the state will come and cart his body away. Someone will shampoo or replace that carpet.

And we'll always get paid.

But we can see the twist in your lips. We see that you don't fully believe us, but since you're not depositing the funds into our account, we hardly care. It is a bit irritating, though, how insistent your growing simper can be.

Hey, guys, we've got another skeptic here.

What if we got the wrong Saben? Isn't that what's uppermost in your mind?

We laugh since it's a natural thing for humans, even killers, to do. Laugh. To laugh like there's no one listening. We'd walked out the door, Saben's body on the floor, and we'd laughed once we got into the vehicle, already smiling on the lawn leading to the sidewalk. It doesn't mean we're sadists, though. Just that we're human, like you, and humans laugh. We laugh, you laugh. Saben would be laughing, we're sure, if he were still alive.

Okay, knock off the simpering. It hardly matters to us, ultimately, whether we'd gotten the correct Saben or not. We got a Saben. The one that had counted for us. The one for whom we'd collected payment.

You should really check out his photos, though. He had skill, talent.

Our talent had been greater. Our collective talent.

The whole Bad Luck Club thing was a joke, of course. Even assassins need to lighten the mood sometimes. We'd just happened to see the bumper sticker for the BLC and couldn't refrain from adopting it as our moniker, our nom de guerre. No one would ever believe that the Bad Luck Club could capably kill anyone. Saben or otherwise. And so we're laughing.

Who were we meant to kill?

Whom?

Who?

Whom?

Which Saben?

We're not grammarians.

We'd received a call from our client. We're not going to disclose whether we'd gotten the correct Saben or not. It's none of your business. It's ours. You'll maybe see us strolling about, separately or en masse, and be unaware what we're about, who we could be looking for, whether it's a Saben or Steven or Kevin or Devin, but we're strolling about just the same.

We got paid. We'll continue to get paid.

Life is short, right? Even without an organization like ours potentially making lives shorter.

You're still simpering. You think you know us, but you'd be wrong. Most of us are vegetarians. We hate the taste of blood. We think Hitler was an asshole, and his paintings were shit.

Go crack a Fanta.

Maybe the Saben who'd we left on his living room floor had said something about his name being Evan. But then why had he opened the door? No, he was the right guy, had his own framed photographs on his walls.

Information's unreliable sometimes, though, right? Like narrators. Like social media. Like a kindly drunk at the bar who's only really trying to get in your pants and your pants are quite full enough, thank you very much.

Blood vessels are full of blood. It justifies their existence as vessels. Those vessels could be squeezing unformed concrete instead. Thick and thicker mediums squeezed through ever shrinking tubes.

The information has got to be right.

Mediums. Media.

Social. Antisocial.

Saben will never know whether he was indeed the Saben we were looking for. Not for his photography. For his life, his blood. He died not knowing. The information could've been as wrong as information could possibly be.

Our information was sound.

Don't try and guilt-trip us. Don't you dare.

We know we got the right Saben because we believe that we did. See, we can cherry-pick, too. It helps to be choosy as an assassin.

We got paid.

That's all that matters. For now.

We'll continue to get paid.

Correct Saben or incorrect Saben.

We got fucking paid. We're not beggars.

Still simpering? How do we sleep at night, you'd like to know? Go ask the accountant. Better yet, go ask Saben or Steven or Kevin or Devin or Evan on the floor of their own home.

We're tired of talking. We're killers, not conversationalists.

We killed Saben. A Saben in a sea of Sabens, but we got one of them, damn it.

You can quit with the smirking. We know where you live. Maybe we'll pay you a visit.

WHY THE ANCIENT EGYPTIANS REMOVED BRAINS THROUGH THE NOSTRILS

Alice went to a funeral.

It was someone she knew, but not someone she loved. Others were there who'd loved the deceased. Alice hoped this to be true, for she felt an unlovable being the saddest possibility of all sad possibilities. And no matter what, no matter how hard she tried, she could never ever love this person only tens of feet away in the casket at the foot of the stairs that led to the altar.

The heart had been left in the body.

Alice had not the heart to care whether the shell peeping up from the antique white lining had a heart at all. This didn't make Alice heartless herself. She had a great big heart for all lovable beings. But this pale nothing in the polished box hardly meant anything to her, even if they'd meant something to the other somebodies inhabiting the spaces and aisles and pews of the church.

So why was Alice even here?

It was expected. She had known this person, and she knew that the other somebodies in the room knew that she'd known them, too. So, she was here. Unsniffling and dry-eyed.

Alice contemplated forever. But not for long.

Someone had come up to her and shaken her hand. She couldn't remember the person's name, but she could remember their position at work, the department to which they belonged, which plate glass along a hall of windows had shielded this person from the rest of the workplace, this person who was now gently and for a bit too long shaking her hand.

This person had bitten their lower lip, maybe because Alice had done the same, humans being repeaters, after all. Alice remained seated, however, while the person who'd shaken her hand had nodded and padded away.

The heart was the center of a person's being.

Alice couldn't move, mummified limbs and strips of linen wrapped tightly around the bench and back of the pew. She wanted to move. She wanted to walk straight out of this funeral, this room, this church, but she couldn't. Not for lack of ability, but for lack of love for this person in the casket. The fact that the others, all the others with flaming love in their hearts for this passed soul maybe were watching was reason enough.

Etch that to a wall, paint it in bright colors.

Alice tried and failed at remembering the magical words, the specific prayers. She'd also failed to bring an amulet for the pharaoh. Some of the others who'd approached the mahogany casket had placed small secret objects deep within the wrapping. Yards and yards of linen. Hundreds of yards, and not one object as offering in Alice's hands or pockets.

In the left pocket of her slacks, the eastern side, she had a folded and unused tissue paper.

In her right pocket she had a stick of gum. Spearmint. She unwrapped the foil and popped the gum in her mouth. She chewed quietly. She could move at least this much.

Alice chewed gum at a funeral.

The Opening of the Mouth ritual had been fully performed, and yet her chest felt hollow. The supine body cavity stuffed with linen and wearing garish eye makeup. Had false eyes been painted on the lids? Alice couldn't, and wouldn't even if she could, get up and see. Awkward resurrection.

Confirmation. Confirmation bias. The dais with the altar empty, unpopulated by preacher or officiator or family member.

Where's the emcee?

No one to pontificate? No one to usher or declaim or aver or simply clear a throat in preface of a declaration of love, maybe? No one and nothing, yet someones were here and something was happening. This wasn't a painting on a wall.

A dead person can speak after the Opening of the Mouth ritual. They can eat. They can chew gum, if they've got it, if they so choose. If they so chews.

Alice knew there was nothing funny about a funeral. Especially when the love that usually spread plumply against her ribcage had up and walked out the funeral, the room, the church, even if Alice's legs were too weak to follow her stridently beating heart. Love. For the unlovable it's unthinkable, unactionable.

There were canopic jars at the ends of every other pew. They were full of livers and stomachs and kidneys and sesame oil and sand and regret and great globs of failure. No hearts, though. And no brains.

The heart was kept in the body, while the brain was pulled and scraped out.

Heartful. Brainless.

Palm wine for the brain cavity, slosh the meat, liquefy all inhibition, tilt the head toward the east, kiss the sun, drain the brain slurry into a clay pot and dump it outside in the dusty streets.

If Alice could just get up. Stand on her two unbroken, nerve-heavy legs.

Alice wiped a crust of natron from her eye. Was that a tear? Had the sun failed to burn up that little pool in the desert? The fluorescents would burn eternally.

Had the person in the casket hurt Alice? Not as such. Not in any conscious or literal way. Some small condescension, to be sure. A passive-aggressive comment here or there. Maybe a scraping tool left mid-excerebration. Would that, now, lead to an infection? Maybe an infection that would go straight to the heart? Who'd be to blame?

Alice coughed at the funeral.

A bit of spearmint and palm wine and embalming fluid slipped past her epiglottis. She choked, tasted mint, and watched bulrushes bloom before her.

She covered her mouth and looked around her. Bitten lips. Slow, very slow nodding. Watery eyes. Maybe, too, she appeared to be crying, weeping for the dead, for the not-so-dearly departed.

We knew you loved him, her, them, they'd say.

Alice knew it was a lie. She'd never loved him or her or them or that manmade mountain of rock and sand against the ever-rising sun.

She scratched at the eastern side of her belly. There could've been a scar there, from something taken that she couldn't remember, but she wasn't lifting her blouse to check. Not while in a church at a funeral with all these lip-biting and eye-watering mourners. She clutched her fly amulet, instead. Lapis lazuli and gold to ward off the biters. This was for her and her alone.

The ethmoid bone can be punctured with a chisel. The tool need not have been fashioned from metal. A sliver of bamboo would do. Or a reed stalk. Or the cold hard finger of a tiny and heartless god. Some god with a heart too tiny to be regarded as a heart by any embalmer. The priests tap-tap at the bone.

All moisture is removed from the body.

Alice hadn't ceased choking and leaking. She secretly slipped some linen strips up under the flesh over her cheekbones. She rubbed her face in natron and sacred cat's piss. She let the sun bake her like clay.

The person in the casket whom Alice didn't love and yet had come to see had not been a very good person, in Alice's estimation. Surely in anyone else's. The mummy had been a blowhard, a bloviator, with a great bovine skull to crack other bovine skulls. She didn't know the names of those around her. Lost to memory, maybe, lost in rites, in the meaningless repetition. The skulls, the people, while the brains turned to a thick stew.

The funeral lasted for seventy days. Surely less than that.

Alice was on her sixty-ninth day and started to get the prickles in her legs. Feeling was returning. Resurrection. The sun had not only hit its zenith, it was slipping down the other side of its transit and spreading its brains all over the Delta plain.

Rising river. Runoff.

Shaky hands with hooked implements could disfigure their appearance. Alice would hate to walk through the Afterlife with a messed-up face. Or without a heart. Or an empty head.

Satin-lined caskets, though. Mahogany. Really?

All the pharaohs were dead. Long since dried out and ground up and used as pigment by painters.

Screw them, Alice said to herself.

Whether she'd meant the deceased or those who were there to honor the deceased or the pharaohs who refused to be disremembered, it was hard to say. Alice, though, had opened her mouth and she'd be damned if she was going to let any of those around her shut it again.

Not for this forgettable sap wrapped in opulence.

So it was a man in the sarcophagus?

Who knows? Who cares? Poor beggar. Shut up.

Alice felt strong enough to stun a cow with a punch, though that'd be the last thing she'd do to the creature, instead patting its flank. She wouldn't hurt a fly. She clutched her amulet again and knew that she — Alice, Alice the uncrying — still had a heart. And she had full use of her brains.

Alice stood up, turned, and left the funeral.

She carried her heart with her through the desert.

WHAT WAS IN THE BOX BY THE SIDE OF THE ROAD

Cartwright played with the scab on his tongue with the edge of a molar. He was driving down the busy four-lane highway. It was late afternoon. Light found the soft spots of all matter and sunk itself into everything. That slight pressure on the scab, the acid wash of light, the grip on the steering wheel phasing into plasma—the culmination of these sensations felt like shadow off the finger of destiny, and that finger pressed ever so slightly into the sweat-soaked t-shirt and flesh and bones beneath that were also turning to plasma.

Cartwright was plasmatic. He was here and there and back. His car squished along the two lanes of the four-way like corn syrup through the line off a blood bag. The rubber in the rolling and steaming tires shifted in and out of solidity. He was a tube of toothpaste, the car the paste, the car now the tube, his body the paste and tube at the same time.

These impressions would instantly form into unbuckled metal and curved glass once the possibility of collapsing into the other cars on the freeway had become a reality. The states of matter in the suspension of entropy.

He was forever. He was as ephemeral as a sneeze.

Cartwright had a brother who went missing in Brazil, just outside of Amazonia, he believed, for whatever that meant. Destiny had already come to the younger of the two fraternal twins. In what form, the older had never discovered. The last he knew of his twin was that he'd rented a car in Curitiba, at the airport.

Maybe that's why he was thinking of his brother now, being in a car, a solid thing, and yet shifting among states of matter, the thoughts themselves colliding and sloshing. The pull of destiny among all these transitory states was undeniable. The slashing rays of the sun continued to sink into everything above the tarmac, into the asphalt, into the soft flesh of the earth beneath, and died a cooling death.

Cartwright engaged the clutch, popping the car out of gear, coasting like heavy bodies coast on water. Both hands to the wheel, now, barely gripping the vinyl, eyes swimming across four lanes.

Something was out there. Something extraordinary. Something for which it would be impossible for Cartwright to avoid. Destiny. Destiny was a carcass on the freeway.

And then it happened.

Cartwright stopped flicking at the scab on his tongue. His teeth clicked together. He didn't want to accidentally bite off the scab mid collision. His tongue stabbed at the bulwark of his teeth, but it was impenetrable.

Wait. Collision?

Cars nervously shook in their lanes. Some swerved into others. Brakes squealed and red lights winked across the melting field. Hungry wolves sensed a soft and shivering body. The carcass. Destiny. Erratic zigzags.

Oh, dear brother, where have you gone?

A woman zipped back and forth along all four lanes, stooping to pick something from the road, zipping again, stooping and grabbing, clutching invisible things to her frail chest, and zipping away again. A bird. A human. A kaon. Dark matter striking xenon. Infinitesimal bits stuck in gelatin after the collision the collision dear brother, the collision.

Cartwright coasted. He didn't panic. He gently merged into the right lane. Cars splayed out before him. The parting of the waters. Horns shattered the air. Pupils exploded. Supernovas sucked themselves into a kiss. Skin set to rip along thin lines of bone.

States of matter were about to become irreparably sundered.

The woman jumped in front of the car before Cartwright. He swerved at the last second to avoid crushing the rear of the car. Blinding the wolf. Red angry eyes popping back open. He'd surely swish past and avoid the woman altogether.

Destiny. It also has red wolf eyes. It laughed in snarls for a second, a half second, a broken atom of a second. The pink tongue flicked and tasted all six flavors of quarks in pieces.

Eyes bulged. Real human eyes. Terrified eyes. They gazed into Cartwright and the expression had melted from fear into a tarpit in which she'd been sinking, in which his car had been skimming. A blackhole spun as he smashed his brakes. He fishtailed. He stood on his brake pedal, hair brushing the headliner above.

He launched grill-first into the gaping maw of destiny. Swallowed whole.

Everything became plasma in that moment.

I see you seeing me seeing me seeing you.

I crush you from existence and our existences intertwine and meld into one form.

I am about to become you. You are about to become me.

Cartwright could smell asphalt hardening. The burn of colossal friction. Brake fluid in the teeth. The scab on the tongue pressing against the roof of his mouth, the ceiling of his car, the pad on the index finger of destiny that had dared race the beams of the sun.

The woman's face solidified and sharpened. She turned and ran across the exit lane, up the small hill to a pharmacy's parking lot with a pizza box in her hands.

Pizza box?

Cartwright checked the mirrors before turning into the lane that led up to the parking lot. The brakes were mud and he had to stand once again on the pedal to come to a complete stop. He glanced in his rearview mirror.

Nothing was backwards. Everything ran forward in time.

He watched the woman deposit the pizza box on the passenger seat of a car, slam the door, enter the driver's side, and peel away. Up on the hill, in the rearview, Cartwright continued to watch, stunned and buzzing, as she unraveled and disappeared into the distance.

Just like his brother had.

Destiny.

Unavoidable, and yet avoiding the fatal impact. He felt the crash, nonetheless, in his chest. The seatbelt was bone, a long human bone, separated and jammed crosswise across his body. He blinked as the memory of red eyes blinked back.

Another car had come down the lane from the hill, from the parking lot, going the wrong way. It skirted Cartwright's flank, skimming the cars in the driving lane going the opposite direction.

Everything through Cartwright's windshield had flipped, wending backward, willing time to reverse all grand collisions and upsets and fatalities, to make all things uncrushable forever.

His brother returned, back from exotic locations with adventures to relate. Theories of infinitesimal bits of matter. Antimatter. Plasmatic whispers.

The car that had passed him parked several feet behind him. A woman, a different woman, had jumped out, pulling a large box with her, setting it to the grass in the berm, backing away with a hand to her chest, and thudding her way back to the car.

Carwright could hear her heart hammering. The blood in his ears thickened. Sludge muffled the sound of the woman's panic.

She jumped back into her car, pulled a U-ey, and raced into the driving lane amid the blaring of horns. Time compressed. Space elapsed.

Cartwright kept checking his rearview. Whether forward or reverse, the information in that slim rectangle was difficult to believe.

He was conscious of how hard his own heart was beating. It matched his breaths. His breaths could fill the sails of a boat on quantum foam and dart prow first into the swirling heart of eternity.

Cartwright's brother. Maybe he was somewhere there in the stream. If he could catch a glance in the rearview of anything more than the cardboard box that had been dumped in the grass off the berm of forever, millennia ago, moments ago, it would be solid enough. Whether forward or behind. Time in flux, time in stasis.

He felt his body accumulating solid objects. Disparate rocks drew closer together. Metal and rubber and glass bent and bubbled in his direction. A center of gravity. The heart of the ocean churning more and more plastic.

The maelstrom had lost its name in the howling, and yet it called to him. From the center a white eye formed, and that white eye watched him like the blind watch all unwatchable things. The eye was a placid sea, unspinning, unhaunted, and it called like only mute beings can call those around them.

Cartwright felt a tugging at his clothes, at his flesh, ready to pitch headlong into the white sea, and the howling of the sea had the sound of his name in it. The seals and gaskets of his car, the bits screwed down but not screwed down enough, wiggled and shook and whistled from the pull of the eye. But it was all deaf, being an eye and not an ear, and heard Cartwright's gasps stuck in his throat like only the deaf can hear terror pulsating membranes and faint hairs.

Should he get out? What would his brother have done? He'd lost himself in a jungle, maybe, but before that he would've exited the vehicle, braced himself against the storm, the white sea, the sun's strafing bullets, and it would've left him just as powerless.

Cartwright was not his brother. He hadn't known what had happened to him. His whereabouts were a mystery. Cartwright, the twin in the rearview, must allow that great unknown, and the violence about him, to seep into his flesh, knife his skin, flay him there and then on the hot asphalt outside the vertiginous sea, if that's what it would take to know, to finally know, to gratefully put the disappearance of his brother to rest.

Where's your brother? the white eye had asked.

A question heard by the insane when they question whether those around them had spoken or not. Only those who've lost their minds can understand the chatter of chaos. Only the sane disbelieve them.

There was a box. He had to see what was inside. A head, a heart, his brother, his brother's killer, his destiny echoing in his head, his heart, the box. While the white eye watched all.

Cartwright, the elder twin, slipped out of the rear-view mirror and exited the car.

Time and space stayed put. It didn't collapse.

He sniffed, since the sun and heat made his nose run. He played with the scab on his tongue while walking toward the box in the grass.

Destiny had heat. At the core was endless fusion.

The box appeared to be an ordinary box, so Cartwright approached it with an ordinary stride, though it felt like a lie, an affectation. His toes met one side of the box and it felt like such an ordinary thing to do. Curiosity became confused with destiny. He had to peek inside. Any ordinary human would do such an ordinary thing.

So he did it. All four flaps spread out.

He looked inside. His molar flicked at the scab.

How does a scab form on the tongue? It's a muscle, not ordinary skin. How can something heal in such a wet environment? What happens when that scab disappears? Does one swallow it while sleeping? Like all the spiders an ordinary human supposedly consumes in very real and ordinary sleep? Like the jungle had swallowed his brother?

Light poured out of the box. The same exact kind of light that had been pummeling his windshield and turning it to plasma.

Forward. Backward.

Cartwright pulled eternity from the box. The head and heart of destiny.

A gun. A card, in fact.

The gun was lightweight. The card was fashioned from lead. Plutonium. A teaspoon's worth of blackhole. The head and heart of density.

The gun was fake. Made of sugar. It broke and crumbled in his hand. He tasted sweet dissolution like only those without the sense of smell can taste it.

The card absorbed all light. Matte gray. Lead. Leaden destiny clutched in his ordinary fingers.

Or you'll never see your brother, in black type.

Cartwright dropped what was left of the disintegrating gun.

He reversed the card.

Saben must die. You must kill him.

Also in black letters. Ink from the blackhole. Hammered steel. Aluminum. Tin. Elements. Everyday elements in his hand.

Cartwright's heart was a hammer and it was an anvil and it was the voice of fate deafened by the hammer blows. He flicked at the scab. A fly landed on his left ear.

Brother.

A whisper. He spun around.

I'm here.

From his car. The trunk. Something was locked inside. Or someone.

The light was so bright, glinting off the back window. Cartwright contemplated the names of stars he knew. He walked over the melting asphalt with the card in his hand. He pulled out his keys. Light danced off those, too, before plunging into the hard metal flesh of his car so recently a lump of plasma. He turned the key and there was a groan. Gas from an opened crypt. Dust and light. Winking white sea. Blinking stars that've already died.

Destiny blinked back.

Brother.

His brother wasn't in the trunk. No one was. Maybe a spirit had been released. There'd been a breeze that whisked by his left ear, flushing the fly from its perch. Maybe the fly was the spirit. Maybe Cartwright himself now was more properly spirit. Shifting states. Maybe he'd hit the woman, or a star, or the great white eye that called to him, though he couldn't make out what it was saying. Cartwright was dumb. His ears had exploded. His eyes swimming with plastic debris in howling chaos. Cartwright was nothing more than air loosely bound up in bone and blood and flesh and the dark memory of what destiny had whispered.

Both eyes blinked. The one eye and the other. Twins. White crashing oceans.

Brother.

The maelstrom of the ocean's center slowly stopped spinning. His eyes adjusted to ordinary things. The trunk of his car was an ordinary trunk with carpet that had never been vacuumed. Loose bits of soil that had once held an alien creature, maybe, or a vampire. A vampire of light amid the rusty tools.

Pierce my heart.

There was a slot in the spot over the spare tire. He inserted the gray metal card with the order to kill Saben.

Who was Saben? Cartwright hadn't the faintest clue. And the gun had disintegrated, anyway.

Nothing happened.

Cartwright tried to extract the card. It was stuck. He was stuck. Maybe his brother had been stuck in time this whole time for all time since the time he'd gone missing. Maybe all this was the final light of his existence, that from distance, like with some stars, had already been extinguished.

Why a vampire? And why of light?

Cartwright closed the trunk lid. A woman was standing there. She froze a second. A strange quark experiencing gravitation. The weak and strong interactions. She placed a shoebox on the hood of Cartwright's car and looked straight through Cartwright. Electromagnetism. She spun and ran away.

Cartwright yelled after her. He almost ran after her, too, but it was too hot. Gravity was too strong. His brakes were shot. His skin felt near to slipping off his bones.

Besides, destiny was calling from everywhere, but nowhere as strong as it was from the cardboard heart of the shoebox.

A cloud blocked the sun, and the world was swallowed in shadow. Cold sweat. Star death. A god blinded to the world that he or she'd created.

He. She. Twins.

All was in shadow.

Cartwright rounded the car and flipped the top of the shoebox back. He looked inside. The veil was pulled across the sky and the angry white eye of destiny burned up the earth, the tarmac, his car and his body and all the cars and all the bodies that were slowly sinking into the pit. The maelstrom in reverse.

He flicked at the scab on his tongue.

There was another card at the bottom of the box. It was paper, not metal. There were words in red ink that couldn't have been his brother's blood. No way.

You may now remove the metal card.

Cartwright looked up. In the distance, at the intersection, waiting for the light to change, maybe, the woman who'd deposited the shoebox stared at him. The white sun stared at him. The white center of the sea. He stared back. At the woman and the sun and the dead eye of the sea.

What is going on? Why going on? When and who?

Where oh where oh where was his brother?

The woman disappeared. Cartwright hadn't noticed when. He went back to his trunk and reopened it. There still wasn't anything there except the unvacuumed carpeting and gray card sticking halfway out the floor.

He removed the card with ease. Still nothing happened. A bathetic hum, maybe. Cartwright shut the lid and held the card against the full glare of the sun. A rainbow limned the edges. The promise of a resolution, maybe.

Ask the beggar, the card now said, still in black ink.

Which beggar? Why? And how would they know any more about what the hell was going on?

Cartwright got back into his car. It was hot. The center of the sun. Solar plexus melting. He pulled the seatbelt over cartilage where there should've been solid bone. Plasma.

The scab in Cartwright's mouth was the only solid thing.

From out of the tar in the distance, at the intersection where the woman had stared at him, grew a black blob. It had stretched from the tarmac and formed into a ball and absorbed all light, just like the gray metal card had done. Or had it been a prism? The blob grew, drew closer — a reverse Doppler effect — hovering the sidewalk then the berm then the grass to stop a few feet over Cartright's windshield.

I am becoming you. You are becoming me.

The blob vibrated in space. It shook out stubs, then limbs. They reached the ground in front of his car. They stretched to the sides. A faced formed from nothing and it was exactly the kind of nothing-face you'd expect a blob to have. Vaguely familiar. Instantly forgettable.

Brother?

But it wasn't his face.

The guy held out his hand to Cartwright and mumbled dead words. Cartwright shook his head, unbuckled his seatbelt, and exited the car.

"You have something for me," the man said.

"Are you the beggar?"

The man shook his fist, but there was nothing in it. He opened his fist and clutched at air.

"I don't have anything for you," Cartwright said.

"Something you were given."

"You mean the card?"

"I know not what you mean."

Cartwright felt sweat roll down his chest and back. He remembered what had been written on the card.

"Who's Saben?"

The man kept clutching his hand. Maybe it was one of the very few movements accorded to a human freshly formed from tar. Maybe they were given only so many motions.

"Give me what I came for."

"Well, then, I'm sorry to say that you came for nothing, because I don't know what you're talking about."

"You have something."

"I've got busted brakes, that's what I've got. I've got sweaty balls and a sweaty back. I've got a whole lot of boxes that are more like Russian dolls without the cuteness. It's not funny and it's kind of pissing me off."

The man didn't blink. Why bother forming eyelids?

"Give me."

His hand still out. He edged closer. The shoebox on the hood of the car started to vibrate now. The man's eyes vibrated in their inky sockets. The box lifted in the air. It drifted toward the man-blob and sunk itself into his chest.

Plasma. Everywhere.

States of matter would never tire of shifting until matter itself ceased to exist.

"Where's my brother?"

"Lost in the jungle," the man said. "In the soil. In a car trunk. Twisting in soil and becoming. Waiting to be awoken. Waiting for the light that slices through all darkness, through the distances of deep time and space." The man's hand was still out. "Give me."

Cartwright patted his pockets. That's where the paper card had been. The card was now gone. He instead pulled out a gun. It wasn't made of sugar. It was solid and rang with destiny. Cartwright was surprised when he'd pointed it at the beggar with a steady hand. The beggar didn't seem surprised. The gun shook in his hand now, but that was only because everything around him was vibrating. He was surprised at how easily the idea of depressing the trigger came to him. Harmless as flicking a fly. A breeze. He fired the gun, and it wasn't by accident, and the thing collapsed in his hand.

Sugar. Stars exploded galaxies away. Violence unrealized.

Cartwright gulped and discovered that he'd clipped and swallowed the scab on his tongue. There was nothing there except muscle and mute surprise.

"Brother."

"I am not your brother."

The man stepped forward again. His shins hit the fender of Cartwright's car and they formed into the fender. His body slid over the hood and splatted into the glass. His hand reached into the cabin. It grabbed at nothing, at everything.

Cartwright flicked at the scab that wasn't there.

He watched the man become the glass and the glass become the man. Flesh to metal, metal to blood and flesh. Melting humans, melting cars, melting earths, from universe to universe, matter and antimatter making an uneasy peace.

What had that woman been picking up from the road? Why had the box been dropped off? And the shoebox? Who was Saben? Where the hell was Cartwright's brother?

Cartwright's car was a box. He stepped inside the box. The box was hot. It shielded him from all possible destinies. Good. Bad. Ones too ugly to contemplate. Ones too beautiful to exist in this melting world.

A large bead of sweat rolled from his chest hair into his waistband. Then another followed another. The slippery slope of plasma.

Cartwright started his car. He pulled onto the main route once the traffic thinned. He braked by letting off the gas. Sometimes he applied his brakes and stood in mud in his car.

A bead of sweat formed on the highway. The grass at the edges. The white lines, the yellow lines. The bead of sweat rolled into shimmering heat waves over the dripping tarmac under the white sun.

Brother.

"You're not in my trunk," Cartwright said to himself.

Brother.

"I'm not pulling over."

Brother.

"I'm tired of boxes. Don't make me look inside another damn box."

Brother, I'm nowhere.

"I know."

Brother, I'm everywhere.

The light. The light outside the windshield. It melts glass. It melts metal. It makes glue of rocks. It makes reality a swirling ocean.

We are the ocean. We are the swirl.

Cartwright's brakes were mud. Plasma.

Solid objects were only necessary to check the endless flow of waters. Liquid kisses, liquid splashes. When a solid object meets another solid object the resulting collision could end the universe, this universe, that universe, the shockwave at the outer edge of any known universe.

Light slashed through Cartwright's windshield. It illuminated exactly nothing. Not anything of substance. Not anything with meaning. Light sunk itself into flesh, into the fabric of the chair, and nothing changed at all.

WHAT WAS IN THE BOX BY THE SIDE OF THE ROAD

Cartwright couldn't know why the boxes existed and why they'd been set in his path to intercept. He couldn't know because he felt the hand of destiny, the finger on that hand pull itself out of his body. He'd watched it slip back out of the car. It had dissolved or dissipated or disintegrated into invisible states of existence. It had told him nothing. It led him only toward confusion.

His brother's name wasn't Saben.

Maybe destiny had accidentally come to the wrong man. Sometimes, maybe, fate can make a mistake, too. Cartwright's brother could've been the intended recipient. The woman could've been merely picking up her own teeth off the tarmac that destiny had knocked straight out her mouth.

Solid objects hitting solid objects.

But though Cartwright couldn't and wouldn't know what had just happened to him, and what had indeed happened to his brother, all those countries way, he still wanted to know what his brother's fate had become.

Brother, which universe have you slipped into?

A jungle of plasmatic possibilities.

It would have to be enough.

WHEN THEY DIED

The plane didn't crash. They didn't die.

There was a dead silence, though, between them.

When they'd landed at PPT, they'd a bit to wait for the flight to Bora Bora. Not Bora Bora, exactly, but the small islet of Motu Mute where the BOB airport was. It took a boat from there to get to the main island.

"We have to get on a boat, too?"

Alan wore consternation better than he wore his own skin. Corrugated consternation. Wrinkles on the forehead and around the eyes.

"You knew this," Ann said. "We went over this before we left North Carolina."

"North Carolina." Alan stared into the horizon and maybe an unflushable turd hung there. "It seems like days ago."

"Two days, in fact." Ann scratched at an eyelid. "If you account for the time difference."

This, however, is the cart before the horse. If people still used horses to lug carts about. Well, the Amish would surely have an affinity for the idiom. One assumes the Amish have their own batch of outmoded expressions that trot by in market wagons while the rest of us gawk from our sleek cars. Jokes about buttons, maybe.

Before this, Alan and Ann had considered the cocktail menu at the airport lounge. The one in Tahiti.

"Fa-ah-ah," Alan had said. "What does that even mean?"

"It's Tahitian."

"Then why's everything in French?"

Ann sighed. Loudly enough for the bartender to think it'd been directed toward him.

They'd been asked if they were ready to order. In English. English.

"But all the signs are in French."

Alan stared at the horizon again. The water was so blue. Impossibly blue. Until that moment, Alan most probably disbelieved anything could be so blue. Except for the water in an airplane's toilet.

"He's waiting," Ann said.

"Oh, yeah." Alan pointed at an illustration of a woman on a can. It wasn't in French. "I'll take the Hinano Tahiti."

"The lager, blond, or amber?"

"Aaahhh . . ."

"Which beer style would you prefer?"

"I don't know. Which one would you suggest?"

"Good Lord," Ann said.

"That depends on the style of beer you like."

All over the world, halfway around the world, right next door even, bartenders are answering this very same question. Some are groaning. Some are smiling. The ones who want the better tips are groaning less and smiling more.

"I'll take the lager," Alan said.

"One Hinano it is."

The bartender had turned to Ann and opened his mouth. Ann was on the verge of opening her mouth, too. In another time, halfway around the world, right next door even, they'd maybe lock eyes, lock lips in a kiss. Who knows?

Or maybe it had just been in Alan's head.

Whatever the case, he beat them both to it. He knew the punchline and blurted it out before the setup of the joke could even be finished. It had nothing to do with buttons.

"The lady will be having the Tahitian Vanilla Punch."

Alan had been smirking the whole damn time.

Pineapple and orange juice. Dark rum, white rum. Tahitian vanilla bean simple syrup. That part's critical. Limes. Vanilla sugar. Ice cubes. Rim the glass with citrus and dip it into the sugar. Stick a slice of orange on the rim.

It did sound good. Amazing, in fact, Ann already knew. But that wasn't the point.

The bartender had spun and went to make one drink and pour another. No other questions asked.

This is what had annoyed Ann. She hadn't cared that this had been a private joke between them. Now if it were something about buttons and zippers . . . But the man ordering the food for the wife and the wife demurely nodding in obeisance, even if it had been only a drink this time, was what had annoyed her. The joke had never been that funny, anyway. It was more of an observance. A curiosity witnessed amongst couples well past middle age and completely unaware of the watchers who'd thought this kind of quaint sexism quietly amusing.

Ann and Alan were smack dab in the middle of middle age. Buttoned to the horizon. In the middle distance of that age, there was still, may always be, that unflushable turd. There was no end to the blue water, stretching beyond human eyesight that had so recently warmed once free of climate control and cabin pressure.

They hadn't shared more than six consecutive words together since. The joke had died an ignoble death. The drinks had been great, though. And goddamn, that Tahitian vanilla really did make a difference. That vanilla punch sky.

Since they hadn't themselves died, in the plane or spread in pieces along the expanse of that impossibly blue water, they'd been forced to share more than six consecutive words having landed at Bora Bora airport with all their buttons intact.

"So now we've got to take a shuttle?"

"Of course, Alan." Ann didn't even blink. "Unless you plan on Jesus-lizarding it over to the island."

Alan headed toward the sign that said Boarding Shuttles for Vaitape.

"Wait," he said. "What about our luggage?"

"The hotel's taking care of it."

"What do you mean?"

"Just what I said."

Alan sighed.

"Ann, would you stop being so short with me? We're supposed to be on vacation."

"La Fin de Bora Bora has a luggage transfer service. We don't need to worry about our bags. They've got them. And they provide the shuttle, too."

"Free?"

"It's part of the whole thing."

Alan scratched at the stubble on his chin. Would the airport's toilets have water as blue as those on the airplane?

"What's La Feen Duh Bora Bora?"

"Jesus, Alan."

Ann headed off toward the shuttles. Alan followed her.

The silence between them resumed. Upon boarding, whilst cruising along the impossible blue expanse, landing at Vaitape, standing on the dock — silence reigned as king and queen. Well, queen first and king stumbling after since she'd been the one to keep inventory on the buttons.

Then what? Electric car rental? A Renault Twizy? An E-Moke? Underwater scooter? What the hell are those, anyway? (Cyborg seahorse-human hybrids?) Ride the back of a blacktip reef shark into the hotel's lobby? Is the lobby just a big pool? Is it just the ocean? A lagoon within a lagoon?

Hell if Alan knew.

Ann knew everything that Alan didn't.

At least that's how it seemed to him. And Ann knew that that was the one thing Alan was always right about.

Once they'd checked in and made it to their room and unpacked and yawned and brushed hair and teeth, they both headed to The Coconut Crab, which was located somewhere within the sprawl of La Fin de Bora Bora.

Better jump in the underwater scooter again. Or grab the dorsal fin of that awful nice blacktip shark. Maybe they'd have sushi on the way. Maybe Mareva would help them. Mareva's the name of the shark. Of course, Ann would be the one to name her.

"On Wednesdays they have Mexican night," Alan said, staring at the menu.

"It's not Wednesday."

"It's not? Bummer."

"We travel halfway around the world and you want to eat Mexican?"

"It says they've got tacos, fajitas, ceviche, guacamole, the works."

"I'm having the Dream of Heaven."

"What's that?"

"The name of the shark."

"Huh?"

"Skip it."

"I don't see Dream of Heaven on the menu."

"Get the Monster Burger."

"Ooh, it's a double decker."

Over her menu, Ann watched Alan come as close as possible to salivating without actually drooling.

"I'm getting a beer, too," he said. "One of those Hinano thingies."

"The lager, blond, or amber?"

"Crap. I don't remember."

"Myself, I'm getting the Mai Tai Roa."

"What the heck's that?"

"A mind eraser."

Alan put down his menu and looked at his wife who wasn't looking at him anymore.

"Come on, Ann. Would you take a look around you?"

He waved his right hand from left to right. "We're in paradise. We came all this way. Let's not spoil it."

Ann put her menu down, too.

"You're right," she said. "I'm tired of fighting."

The Coconut Crab was on the beach. They were sitting in wooden chairs on rockers, for however they'd work on loose sand, with striped cushions like the flanks of tropical fish. A complete arc of the lagoon spread out, open aired, unwalled. The ceiling was of timber and thatched leaf roofs held together by bush poles and coconut fibers. An affectation of an underwater bungalow, though it was only over the sand.

Ann had done her research. Alan couldn't even remember the name of the hotel they were staying at. Or hadn't until they'd gotten to the Bora Bora airport.

There were other names for the sharks.

Mahana. Flower.

Raiana. Starry sky.

Tapairu. Royal dancer.

Vaipoe. Water pearls.

Ann knew them all by name. She'd petted their dense flanks. She'd kissed the snouts only inches away from the teeth. She'd rubbed the pectoral fins. She stared into their dead and peaceful eyes that held the middle distance and the middle distance only.

"This is nice," Alan said.

"It is."

"Just wish it was Wednesday." Alan rubbed his belly. "Could really go for some tacos about now."

Ann didn't reply. She pretended to scan the menu on the table. She waited for the server to arrive.

The server showed up shortly as proof that he hadn't died. The cold hand lay calm yet ready on the pole in Charon's plane or shark or underwater scooter.

A question of food was asked.

Ann smiled. Alan had opened his mouth and let his teeth bite on tropical breezes.

"I'll have the Ahi Red Tuna Sashimi with a Mai Tai Roa," she said.

Finer details were honed. Courtesies exchanged. Alan still had his mouth open.

"And my man-friend will be having the Monster Burger with a Hinano."

"Excellent."

The server collected the menus from the table and headed off.

Alan, mouth closed, looked confused.

"How does he know which Hinano to get?"

Ann shrugged. "You got the burger. I think it was obvious which beer."

"You think?"

Ann played with a button on her shirt. "Dead certain."

He spread a grin as wide as the lagoon.

"I don't mind you ordering for me," he said.

"Yeah, well, you're still not getting tacos."

Now Alan shrugged. "There's always Wednesday."

Mareva, the shark, turned upside down in the ocean.

Alan kept smiling, like a beggar with a fresh twenty-dollar bill and the future prospect of beer.

Ann let go of her button. She could just die.

WHEN THEY DIED

HOW I KNOW I'M NOT A GOD

One of Twelve in a Twelve-Woman Orgy.

Lewis knew the band name was a mouthful, but he wasn't going to tell Lauren that. She'd kick him, he knew. That title was his fantasy, not hers, goddamnit. Misappropriated fantasy.

Alas.

Faux Leaf Clover.

Lewis had floated this idea to disabuse her notion of nullifying his own fantasy. There's no way Lauren would be willing to let him be one-twelfth of a rutting and sucking endeavor. He'd have to become a woman first, anyway, for any actuality to fall in line with the band name, with his stolen fantasy. What if Lauren was part of the remaining eleven, considering all things equal? Still no?

Well, it was worth a try. Lewis didn't have that big of a dick, anyway, for all that would matter in a lesbian orgy.

Eleven bicurious women plus one, please. So read the response card to the invitation.

Let's change the topic. Lewis is drooling.

Lauren had the idea of taking a very common three-leaf clover and tying one petiole from another onto it to fashion a four-leafed clover. A faux-leafed clover, had been Lewis' riposte.

On one of their walks, while hunting for four-leaf clovers, they'd wandered into a flurry of miniature helicopters, about twenty or so dragonflies, zipping up and down and all around the open field. It was a park named after . . . well, originally a Confederate officer or an instrumental member of the group that had started that riot over a century ago. Had it been renamed? Did it even matter?

Of course it mattered.

Both Lewis and Lauren knew this.

The magic of a veritable dragonfly Bonnaroo hummed around. Sooty snowflakes with intention. You could almost grab them if they'd let you. Since they're the most accurate hunters on the planet, it's hardly likely.

Lewis and Lauren were also aware of this.

Right now, Lewis should be home reading that Haruki Murakami book he'd started something like three weeks ago. He'd barely made it halfway. Not that he didn't like it—it was just one of those books that demanded uninterrupted attention followed by bouts of contemplation. Like a philosophy text. And there were the dragonflies to consider.

Why was Lauren even renaming a band that had never been fully formed in the first place? In fact, there were never more than one and a half members. The one you know. The half member was a cousin of Lauren's in Meadville, Pennsylvania—states away—and that cousin was in love with the idea of leaving Meadville, complaining about the city, the entire state, and yet never leaving.

Love is weird.

Such as it is.

One thing in a series of things that illuminated the fact to Lewis of how he was not a god. Or Lauren, in this case, with the unmaterialized band and ever-shifting band name.

If we were to stick with Lewis, his most immediate failure at deicide was not having sex with multiple women at the same time. It had always been one and only one. Sometimes not even that, but we shall leave solo endeavors behind the shower curtain where they belong. A true god could whip up a horny harem out of air, heavy with a heat index well beyond any mortal's survivability, and screw like Zeus amidst a flock of swans.

How about that, Lauren? Lewis had asked.

Flock of Swans sucks, she'd said. And a group of swans is called a bevy.

That section with the dude eviscerating the cats and eating the hearts, though, in the novel Lewis hadn't finished . . . Man, that was messed up.

Messed Up? Good band name? No?

Such as it is.

Another instance of how Lewis knew he wasn't a god was in how he couldn't—could never, in fact—blow a bubble from bubble gum. He'd tried. Over and over and over until his lips hurt. The eagle gnawing on Prometheus' guts day after interminable day and only causing greater and prolonged torture. Something like that.

Fuck it. Who needed to snap bubbles from bubble gum, anyway? It was such a human thing to do. Not god-like in the least.

There was a brewery from the mountains of North Carolina that had opened a satellite location in Doverton. Lewis and Lauren would hit this place whenever the urge to beat the crap out of a ping pong ball took them. The beer wasn't as good as the surrounding breweries. The beer had less pull than the bank of ping pong tables. Or tennis tables, I guess, to obviate any offense. Wait, hadn't ping pong come from Mandarin? Enough of table tennis.

Such as it is.

I myself, the narrator here, realize how like Vonnegut of a thing it is for me to repeat a phrase such as "such as it is". It's one of the ways in which I know how I'm not a god.

Such as it is.

However, both Kurt V's twelfth book and mine were about a painter, so there's that similarity. A kind of symmetry, at least. A godlikeness of sorts.

I'm with Lewis, though. Jesus over troubled waters, I'd also love to be the twelfth part of a twelve-woman orgy.

Eh. What are you going to do? I'd probably get a cold sore. And Lewis would have a new band name to pitch to Lauren once he'd thrust the shower curtain back into place.

Cold Sore? No?

A few blocks up and over from that field with the dragonflies, Lauren and Lewis noticed an empty box trailer on rusted stands sitting in an unused parking lot. Not completely unused and empty since a backpack rested on the very back ledge of the trailer. Light never made it past the threshold. The darkness within kept all secrets hot and moist. Just imagining the heat index on that makes me woozy.

Whose backpack? A beggar's, maybe?

Later, Lewis alone had passed this same nearly abandoned lot with the nearly abandoned box trailer. The backpack had disappeared. The trailer had been stuffed to the gills with used tires. Did they go all the way to the front, to the cab? It is the front, not the back, with trailers, right? Kind of like house-left and stage-right being the same thing.

Such as it is.

To the gills, though. As if the trailer were a blacktip shark.

The fact that Lewis didn't know whether the back of the trailer was really called the front or the back is another way that Lewis knew he wasn't a god. It's all about perspective, right?

Such as it is.

They'd had a bullet pass through the back of their house one night. A week and a half passed before they'd noticed the hole. But when it'd first happened, that week and a half prior, they'd both heard metal clattering to the floor. Lewis had investigated and found nothing. No fallen pictures or cans of peas or pruners hanging from a Command strip on the wall of the pantry. (The pruners had fallen months ago.) Lauren had noticed what she'd thought was a spider as a very real crack in the wall, and when she'd teased it apart, a very real hole in the plaster. Their investigation took them outside where they'd discovered a burrow through the wood siding. It wasn't the work of carpenter bees.

Where the hell was the bullet?

Lewis couldn't find it in the wall of the pantry. It hadn't smashed an appliance or can of Coke Zero. The hole in the box with the rolls of garbage bags had been caused by the pruners falling those months ago. Lewis had emptied the upended box to find the bullet. He pulled things from the pantry floor into the hallway.

Lo! saith Prometheus, there it is.

A 9mm or .380 caliber bullet on the floor.

If Lewis had been standing at the back of the house when the bullet went through the wall, he'd have gotten it in the jaw. If it had been Lauren, she'd have been struck in the temple.

Such as it is.

Lewis spent way too much money on beer. It wasn't just the alcohol, he'd say, it was about the connections, about running into acquaintances, talking with strangers, hanging with friends. No way it was all just self-medication. Well, sometimes it was, when the base of Lewis' shoulder blade buzzed from repetitive and heavy lifting in what felt like 110-degree heat. That goddamn warehouse.

Lauren drank her fair share of beer, too. Lewis would point this out, but she'd be quick to reply that she didn't drink nearly as much as Lewis and usually only when he was drinking.

Lewis knew this to be true. His back really did hurt, though. It indeed was brutally hot on the ladder to the fourth shelf in the warehouse. It could be worse. He could've been hooked on opiates.

Hooked on Opiates? Will that one work, Lauren? No?

The bottle-conditioned Saison at Huxley's, though. Hoo boy. Even Lauren had to admit it was liquid crack.

Wait. Hold on. You know it. Say it.

Liquid Crack.

Say it again.

Liquid Crack.

One more time, and put your damn buzzing back into it.

LIQUID CRACK.

That's the spirit.

Lauren's having second thoughts. Maybe the band name's glamorizing, or minimizing, something that shouldn't be glamorized or minimized.

Such as it is.

The fact that Lewis would sometimes drink too much and feel guilty about it the next day and fly straight(ish) for the next couple of days is another instance of Lewis' lack of godhood.

Viking gods got drunk, though.

Jesus turned water to wine.

The Romans had bacchanalias.

Noah got pissed and passed out naked in a tent.

Drunkenness of Noah is a painting. A god hadn't painted that. He was human. And I bet that Italian dude drank goblet after goblet of wine.

Such as it is.

To be fair, though, it's far easier to make a list of things proving one's lack of godness than it is to try and drum up anything even smacking of self-divinity.

There's pooping, for one.

Loss of memory.

Communicable diseases.

Tinnitus.

Worn out knees.

Weak enamel.

Alcoholism.

Memory loss.

Club feet.

Hangnails.

Night blindness.

Allergy to water.

Acne.

Sunburns.

Memory loss.

Halitosis.

Drooping eye.

Drifting eye.

Styes.

Astigmatism.

Color blindness.

Memory loss.

Hammer toes.

Tennis elbow.

Bursitis.

Morgellons.

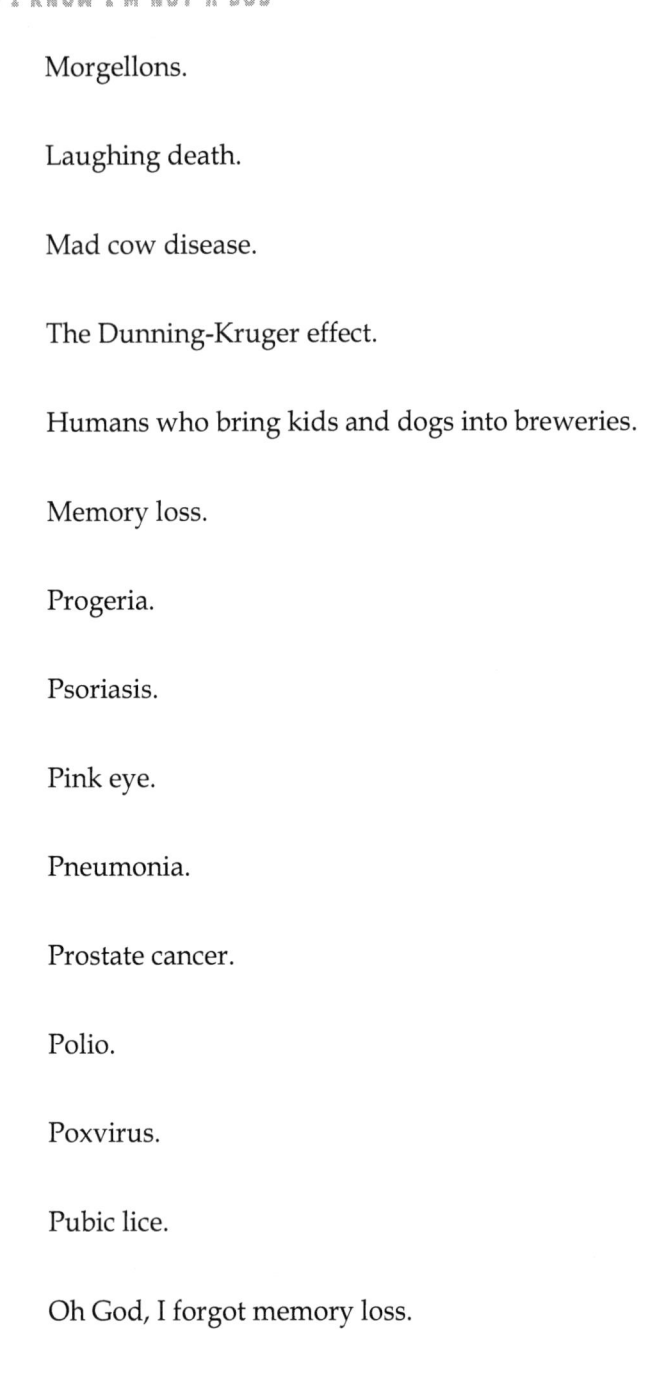

Laughing death.

Mad cow disease.

The Dunning-Kruger effect.

Humans who bring kids and dogs into breweries.

Memory loss.

Progeria.

Psoriasis.

Pink eye.

Pneumonia.

Prostate cancer.

Polio.

Poxvirus.

Pubic lice.

Oh God, I forgot memory loss.

A list of things of how I know I am a god?

. . .

One minute.

. . .

I'm thinking.

. . .

Maybe I need help on this.

. . .

Lewis says that it's his daily ability to take an extraordinarily large shit and barely ever need to wipe. Pooping. That's on the non-god list. Sorry, Lewis.

Lauren says it's how she can create songs out of thin air. Really? That mockingbird over there or there or even that one atop the utility pole can sing far better tunes from a bigger repertoire. And birds can fucking fly. No, Lauren. No dice. Points for trying.

What was that Italian painter's name?

Giovanni Bellini. That's it.

Ah, so my godness is my memory.

Loss of memory.

I remember now.

Bummer.

Such as it is.

I'm looking over a faux-leaf clover.

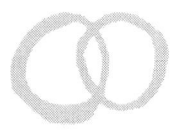

WHAT THAT SOUND WAS

There were two benches facing each other. In each bench sat a person. On the left, a man. On the right, a female. The sexes have nothing to do with the ensuing story. The directions, right and left, don't matter either except from the vantage these directions can be determined; namely, looking from the sidewalk, splitting the space between the benches, with the multi-tiered parking garage in the background.

Each person on their respective bench didn't matter, either. Not in an existential sense, of course, since whether the man and/or the woman mattered existentially was open to free-flowing debate by any philosophy major or marijuana afficionado.

Neither person was into philosophy, academically speaking, and neither had imbibed THC in years. Well, contact highs and armchair philosophizing aside.

The reason that it mattered that these two were sitting in opposing and facing benches was that they wore contrary teams on their shirts. Not sports, good God, no. Not that.

The man's black t-shirt declared TEAM HUMAN in bold white letters. The woman's was a white tee and in black letters said TEAM ANIMAL.

The color of the t-shirts also doesn't matter. Or that of the lettering.

The teams they chose for themselves, though, or the teams that had chosen and supplied them with the t-shirts, are the most important thing of all. Not the teams, as such. The fact that they represented opposing teams.

It wasn't raining. Else, the two wouldn't be on their respective benches. It had rained, however, no more than two hours earlier. The benches had been faintly damp. The man had taken a spare shirt from his backpack and wiped the seat. The woman had employed a napkin snatched from her purse to the same effect.

The fact that neither of their posteriors were wet, or damp even, also doesn't matter. Of course, to the man and woman, the very fact of their dryness was of utmost importance. For the sake of this tale, though, we can wholly and truly assure you that it doesn't.

And yes, we're fully aware of just how much we're telling you that is of no importance. We beg you to bear with us.

To be truthful, the fact that one person (the man) wore a TEAM HUMAN shirt while the other (the woman) had on TEAM ANIMAL was a falsehood. Not an outright lie, exactly, since it's still useful as metaphor. Apparently both parties were acquainted well enough with each other to know that the one was for HUMANs and the other for ANIMALs.

The fact that they knew this may be of importance to the story.

Prior information. Preconceived notions. Predetermined arguments only seconds from blooming in that space between the persons on the benches.

TEAM HUMAN doesn't have to carry around plastic bags in which to hold the pet's scooped feces.

TEAM ANIMAL doesn't have to wipe a miniature human's ass.

TEAM HUMAN doesn't have to stop every three seconds for their child to piss on the neighbors' flowers the whole way down the block.

TEAM ANIMAL doesn't throw rocks at windows.

TEAM HUMAN doesn't dig up the mulch around the rose bushes.

TEAM ANIMAL doesn't crash their three-wheeler into the fender of their owner's car.

TEAM HUMAN doesn't jump all over strangers whenever they come to visit.

TEAM ANIMAL doesn't sass its elders.

TEAM HUMAN likes hugs.

TEAM ANIMAL curls up in your lap.

TEAM HUMAN doesn't need led along by a leash.

TEAM ANIMAL begs to differ.

TEAM HUMAN has their own opinions.

TEAM ANIMAL knows this all too well.

TEAM HUMAN doesn't bark all night long.

TEAM ANIMAL doesn't cry and cry and cry for its binkie. TEAM ANIMAL doesn't even know what a binkie is.

TEAM HUMAN doesn't scratch up the velveteen sofa.

TEAM ANIMAL didn't break the lamp. Not this time. That was totally TEAM HUMAN.

TEAM HUMAN wishes TEAM ANIMAL would stop whining already.

TEAM ANIMAL wishes that TEAM HUMAN would stop pulling at its little peter and go to the bathroom, for crying out loud.

TEAM HUMAN says, You mean barking out loud.

TEAM ANIMAL doesn't get TEAM HUMAN's humor.

TEAM HUMAN can carry on conversations.

TEAM ANIMAL gets it all from anal glands.

TEAM HUMAN says that TEAM ANIMAL should more properly name themselves TEAM CANINE.

TEAM ANIMAL laughs because animals can laugh.

TEAM HUMAN tells them to go fetch.

TEAM ANIMAL stares with a cat's unshakeable indifference.

TEAM HUMAN won't eat their loved one's face when they die since the survivor can get their own damned food.

TEAM ANIMAL says they hate the taste of TEAM HUMAN.

TEAM HUMAN composes poetry.

TEAM ANIMAL can literally HOWL. Suck on that, Ginsberg.

TEAM HUMAN prefers the Romantic era.

TEAM ANIMAL says romance is for the birds, and TEAM ANIMAL would never put birds in cages.

TEAM HUMAN has flown around the world.

TEAM ANIMAL says they went to space first.

TEAM HUMAN cites the fact that they're the ones who built the rockets with their very real opposable thumbs.

TEAM ANIMAL says they can stick that opposable thumb up their booster nozzle.

TEAM HUMAN laughs.

TEAM ANIMAL bares its teeth.

TEAM HUMAN tells TEAM ANIMAL to lighten up.

TEAM ANIMAL tells TEAM HUMAN to fill the water bowl, for Christ's sake.

TEAM HUMAN wants to be loved and can communicate that need.

TEAM ANIMAL nuzzles and wants petted.

TEAM HUMAN was given dominion over TEAM ANIMAL by authority of the Bible.

TEAM ANIMAL doesn't recognize that authority. TEAM ANIMAL also wants to know what a Bible smells like.

TEAM HUMAN says a Bible smells like leather. That is to say, that a Bible smells like TEAM ANIMAL's brethren flayed, dried out, stretched, and glued to paper.

TEAM ANIMAL accuses TEAM HUMAN of being the dirtier animals.

TEAM HUMAN shrugs and says that it is what it is.

TEAM ANIMAL doesn't use tautology.

TEAM HUMAN swears it'll teach TEAM ANIMAL a lesson with the nose of a balled-up magazine.

TEAM ANIMAL reminds TEAM HUMAN that since TEAM ANIMAL doesn't have opposable thumbs, it has no use for periodicals.

TEAM HUMAN calls TEAM ANIMAL a Communist.

TEAM ANIMAL replies that it never made a five-year plan.

TEAM HUMAN calls TEAM ANIMAL a fascist.

TEAM ANIMAL concedes that it's a dog-eat-dog world. Even for cats.

TEAM HUMAN spins "Cat Scratch Fever".

TEAM ANIMAL is okay with OK Computer.

TEAM HUMAN buries their dead and says prayers and sheds tears.

TEAM ANIMAL bays at the moon.

TEAM HUMAN shouts, I knew it!

TEAM ANIMAL accuses TEAM HUMAN of destroying the planet.

TEAM HUMAN points a finger at TEAM ANIMAL and points out how they're the ones that roll in dead things and excrement.

TEAM ANIMAL says that TEAM HUMAN doesn't understand them.

TEAM HUMAN says, Heel! Heel!

TEAM ANIMAL winds its leash around TEAM HUMAN's ankles to trip their would-be masters.

TEAM HUMAN repeats, Heel! Heel!

TEAM ANIMAL circles itself and sniffs a fresh new ass.

TEAM HUMAN scoffs.

TEAM ANIMAL growls.

A silence blooms like a flower between the benches. TEAM FLOWER pops out its head and says nary a word since plants can't speak. Both humans and animals know this.

An immutable fact.

The ineluctable modality of the . . .

Barking?

Speaking?

Building?

Rutting?

A communication through scent.

A communication through sound.

Wait! What was that? That sound there.

TEAM HUMAN turns its head.

TEAM ANIMAL pricks up its ears.

If a tree falls in the forest and TEAM HUMAN isn't there to hear it, does it still make a sound? TEAM ANIMAL is well aware of exactly what a forest smells like, whether trees have fallen or not.

But none of this matters.

The only thing that does matter — and even on this fact both TEAMS can't agree — is what the hell that sound had been.

TEAM HUMAN swears it was a baby. A human baby. The cry was muted and must've come from that brick-squared, plastic-topped trashcan on the corner. TEAM HUMAN would swear to this. TEAM HUMAN almost wants to get up, but the clouds are gathering ever grayer and threaten to rain in torrents all over the benches, making very real and human posteriors more than merely damp.

TEAM ANIMAL would bet its tail that that sound had been a kitten in distress, somewhere in the bushes lining the sidewalk just before the parking garage in the backdrop. Meow meow meow. More than three times, but TEAM ANIMAL bets that TEAM HUMAN gets the point. At least this, surely.

It's a baby.

It's a kitten.

Baby.

Kitten.

WHAT THAT SOUND WAS

Nonetheless, we know something is in distress. That thing—for it is definitely a "thing" outside the dry benches holding both TEAMs HUMAN and ANIMAL and their dry and useless discourse—is coming from beyond the bushes and trashcan. On the periphery, as it were.

To HUMANs. To ANIMALs.

Now, we can promise without hesitation that none of this back and forth matters the slightest. The sides, the teams. The shirts and benches. Not even the trashcan or bushes. It's all, saith the Preacher, Vanity! Vanity!

We believe that vanity may be the ultimate undoing of TEAM HUMAN. And since TEAM ANIMAL doesn't even have vanity in its aromatic lexicon, it is also doomed.

We're all doomed. Both TEAMs HUMAN and ANIMAL.

Well, some of us, anyway. Some humans, and some animals.

What that sound was . . .

To be on the up-and-up about this, let us let the beggars, the homeless, the dispossessed speak for themselves:

No thank you.

This had been spoken by a man on a bench to the left of the man of TEAM HUMAN. He seemed breathless. He was missing teeth. He labored at removing his blue sneakers and then his socks, resting the heels on top of the sneakers, himself huffing and sitting back against the bench. The man's legs seemed a uniform width from calves to ankles, as if he'd suffered from gout. The toenails were long and jagged.

Another man sat opposite him, splayed out on the brick-lined surface past the sidewalk that separated himself from the man puffing on the bench. He had a backpack between his legs. He wore black boots, so his feet hadn't gotten wet when it'd rained earlier. The brick he sat upon was warm and dry. An umbrella was secured within the loops of the backpack.

The man on the bench had wet feet still, hence his airing them out. His name had been asked of him but he hadn't answered, instead looking away, breathing heavily. The man on the ground had given his own name.

None of this really matters except for the man's answer. It was authentic. Almost without thought. He'd declined an offer of an apple as the man on the ground started biting into one.

No thank you.

The man on the ground said he worked at a warehouse and could get a pair of boots for the other man at no charge, remarking the wetness of the sneakers, socks, and wrinkled feet. All he'd need was the man's shoe size.

No thank you.

The man on the bench fumbled with a zipper on his bookbag, also blue, on the bench and gave it up with a deep exhalation. Thankfully, the rain had taken some of the humidity out of the atmosphere.

The man on the ground stood up, went to the trashcan—a different trashcan from the one on the other side of the woman for TEAM ANIMAL—and tossed in the apple core. He extracted bills from a front pocket of his backpack before slinging a strap over his shoulder. He went to the man on the bench, holding out the wad of bills. It was only five dollars, but it was something, at least.

The man shook his head, looking away, breathing deeply.

No thank you.

The man standing shrugged, crimped his lips, stuffed the wad into his jeans and said:

I walk past here every Saturday. If you ever need anything, you can stop me. I'll be here.

The man scratched at his wrist where a faded hospital bracelet hung loosely. He'd never looked the standing man in the eyes.

No thank you.

The standing man walked away with his backpack of apples and pocketful of ones. Maybe there were more than five bills. It doesn't matter. None of this does. Except that he'd walked past TEAM HUMAN and TEAM ANIMAL and neither of them seemed to notice his passing. To be fair, he himself hardly noted the man and woman on their benches. Maybe he was still preoccupied with the man with the missing teeth and wet feet. What shoe size? Would he have had trouble managing the apple with the remaining teeth?

No matter whether it mattered or not, the man walking with the backpack seemed a bit down, face staring at the cracked concrete, for having failed a failed man. Maybe. We don't really know for sure. We don't really know anything.

But there'd been that noise. Again, piping up from the bushes just before the parking garage.

That's definitely a baby, TEAM HUMAN said.

No way, said TEAM ANIMAL. That's totally a kitten meowing.

A beggar, a homeless person, a dispossessed soul, spoke from the bushes, maybe having grown out of and separated themselves from the greenery. The beggar's gender is of no importance. That they'd spoken, though, may have import. What'd been said in the voice of a human baby and meowing kitten was:

Nothing intelligible.

The homeless mumble. Often, they are reluctant to ask for anything.

The man with the backpack, having rounded the benches with TEAMs HUMAN and ANIMAL, approached the man in the green periphery. The homeless can often be found on the edges. The periphery of everything. The man with the backpack found himself also skirting these margins.

There-but-for-the-grace-of-God-go-I kind of thing, maybe.

We don't go there, though. Not into the thickets. We're watchers. We observe and record the events and dialogue. Glorified stenographers in glorified bodies.

Maybe we're in space, outer space, hovering like a swirling hole in the invisible fabric of that space plus time plus distance plus heartbreaking human and animal need. Maybe we float in air with the dragonflies—not pulling them in; more like gently sending them into spins. The dance of wingéd nature, swirled by the cosmos, a paint stick in a paint can. What romance were we painting? Among other things, this story, this event, this exchange of the beggar and the backpacker.

The beggar, though, hadn't asked for a thing.

The backpacker sat on the curb next to the beggar, having asked permission.

One commonality amongst the homeless is their overwhelming body odor. We still can't flush that from our nostrils, and we weren't even sitting on the ledge with the backpacker. The iced matcha latte we'd gotten later, blocks away, failed to cover the stench.

The homeless man, having no home and no access to a bathroom, could hardly have his horrible body odor held against him. We the observers, however, carry all the fault in the world for merely watching and remaining so callous while failing at drowning that stench of homelessness with overpriced beverages.

For shame, TEAM HUMAN. Eh, we're not strictly human, though, so the fault's not entirely at our feet. We're cosmologically indifferent.

The homeless man's name was Tanner.

The backpacker's name is not important.

Another commonality amongst the homeless are their long and yellowed fingernails. Nail clippers are a rarity in the hollows of a homeless person's bag. Even the backpacker hadn't a pair on him, though his pared nails were evidence to the fact that he had access to a bathroom. He smelled of sandalwood, so he most probably had his own house with a bathroom with a handcrafted dish to hold the bar of soap.

Tanner said he'd run away from home when asked by the backpacker why he was there on the periphery of the parking garage. Not there existentially, but there for real, in the hot sunshine, outside the river of humans and animals.

You won't catch the homeless biting their nails They know where their hands have been.

When asked, Tanner said he'd come from Myrtle Beach, and that he'd been forced from the city by the city. He'd ended up in Doverton. On this ledge in Doverton.

The backpacker gave Tanner his ones and apologized he couldn't do more. He handed over an apple. Tanner stowed the bills with care in a wallet, the apple in his bag.

A car pulled along the side of the road, past the greenery, the curb, the benches, the sidewalk, the bricks, the lamppost. A man jumped out of the vehicle and strode through these boundaries, coming up to both men sitting on the ledge with two paper bags and two bottles of water. The man asked them if they wanted PB & J sandwiches.

No thank you, said the backpacker.

Tanner took a bag and water. The man gave him the other bag and water and told him to take care.

That was awful nice of you, the backpacker said to the man as he passed back through the boundaries to his vehicle. The car drove away.

Neither TEAM HUMAN nor TEAM ANIMAL had noted any of this. What they'd noted, as you can surely guess by now, hadn't mattered more than an apple core tossed in the dustbin.

Maybe I should see if the baby in the trash is okay, TEAM HUMAN said.

Maybe I should see if the little kitty is homeless and wants to come home with me, TEAM ANIMAL said.

The backpacker told Tanner that he didn't know of a place where Tanner could stay, but that he'd ask some friends that night when he went out.

Where are you staying now?

There are some churches that let you use their stoops.

Is that where you sleep?

Sometimes there, sometimes on benches.

What if it gets cold?

It's summer.

Summer will end, though.

Tanner, the young homeless man, shrugged.

I'll come back through tomorrow after I talk to my friends.

Tanner nodded.

The backpacker stood up, wished Tanner luck, and walked somewhere well out of sight of TEAMs HUMAN and ANIMAL.

We know where the backpacker went to, but it's no business of ours to tell you. Follow him yourself. Go downtown and sit on a bench not occupied by a beggar. Bring some apples, maybe, or PB & Js. Change a ten for ones and hand them out and not buy that matcha latte instead. Don't go drink with friends at craft breweries since you'll only forget to ask those friends about where a homeless man can find shelter. Never ask Tanner his name. Close your mouth, stop up your nares when striding past the young runaway with the long fingernails and ungodly reek.

Complain about the city not cracking down on the beggars. Why don't they get a job, already? Step around a dog turd on the concrete some poor representative of TEAM ANIMAL had failed to bag. Turn up your nose at PB & Js. Walk into a cocktail bar and order a drink that you'll complain is overpriced. Complain about the state of the government. Complain about the city parking. Get indignant at the beggars balling their fists when you step out of your SUVs. Smack your palm. Get worked up. Get worked up about nothing. Grind anthills between cracks in the sidewalk with the heels of your loafers, your sandals, your fancy shoes. Complain about the sun. Complain about the rain. Complain about the drizzle during sunshine and never note how odd a thing it is to witness sunshine rain. Complain about that homeless man's smell, God, the stench. Complain that the matcha latte's too sweet. The hazy IPA too bitter. The deconstructed PB & J at the bourgie bistro could've used more peanut butter. Go off on a tangent about how crunchy peanut butter is an abomination. Never stop walking until you're safe at home. Never notice the carpenter bees burrowing holes in the gate to your backyard's privacy fence. Complain about your neighbor's weeds climbing over your fence. Rail against the military jets that drown out all sound, even when you can't see them. Complain about masks coming back with the new COVID variant. Yell your head off about the government, the goddamn government not stopping the flood of immigrants with their spread of future and unknown variants. Bitch about Biden, bitch about Obama while you're at it. Say that Trump was a dumbass, and Bush not much better. Believe you're better than anyone, more deserving, that you know more about what's really going on. Share those beliefs with those who bother to hang with you, those who aren't redolent of body odor, those who are fresh with green tea and oat milk and laundered clothes. Bellow at the neighbor's grandson who's pulled the head off a gladiolus. Wave angrily at cars driving too fast down your street, the street with your house that holds a special room, two special rooms, in which to get clean. Turn a blind eye to strangers, angels unawares. Turn deaf ears to babies and mewing kittens. Order t-shirts online and have them shipped within two days. Bitch when they arrive a day late. Put those shirts on. Claim your team. Choose your tribe. Forget what we've said, what we've shown you. Wear that shirt with undiluted pride. Nod at another wearing the same shirt. Identity. Tribal pride. Bump fists, but not with the beggars. Ball up wads of paper and toss them in the bin with the apple cores. Waste your time. You've got the weekend. Waste your money. You've earned it. Waste your life. It's your privilege. Consider it the highest goal to which one can aspire.

Do all this.

You've got nothing else to do. You've got nothing to do at all.

Forget the damn beggars.

You never really wanted to know what that sound had been, anyway.

Neither had we, and we watched it all happen.

In your city of indifference. On your empty benches. Your hearts full of blood that you keep all to yourselves.

We don't even have hearts. Or blood.

We have eyes. And brains to process the information.

God, that stink, though.

Was it from them or you or us?

Ask the baby. Ask the kitten.

You'll get the same answer.

But none of it will matter.

Tanner, though, disagrees. Both his hands are balled around a PB & J sandwich. He chews and swallows and wipes his lips with the back of a hand. He looks straight at us and knows we're watching. He's also aware that we don't care.

Before he takes another bite, he says:

Of course it fucking matters.

WHAT THAT SOUND WAS

WHAT MATTERS TO US

We were going to leave this space for you to fill out. But since it's highly unlikely that you'd bother, we've decided to waste this space ourselves.

You may remember us. We're the observers.

We are not material. We literally are not made of matter. We are energy, and we can use that energy to "gaze" in whichever direction we choose.

The direction doesn't matter. What we see does.

Though we are not matter, we can use our energy to manipulate matter, ever so slightly, even if we employ this subtle power rarely. Observing is difficult enough. The telling, the relating of what we've seen to you beings of matter, is more difficult still. Through the concentration of our energies, we are writing this to you now.

What we say may not matter to you. It matters a great deal to us.

We could've let Tanner, the homeless man from the previous story, have the last word. He could've spoken for us, in part. However, being matter—to you who may not think he matters whatsoever—he can't fully speak for us since he's caught in his own predicament, his own street-stained skin. Mortal flesh, mortal bones, feet to concrete.

Tanner had said what he'd needed to say, and we thought it fitting. We also believe that his statement had worth, weight, substance. What he'd said mattered.

We've watched your species since you broke from the great apes. We've seen you progress, proliferate, pummel, proselytize, ponder, and then doubt that there was anything worth pondering about. Ultimately, that willful slip back into a lower state of consciousness is why we're here saying what we're saying. Before you become apes once again.

It matters to us.

You've read by now, or maybe not, the collation of scientific papers stating your planet's inevitable heating up until 2050. No matter what you do, it won't matter regarding that fact. You can completely halt your worst atrocities against your home planet and you'll still get hotter and hotter for another thirty years.

And that's the best-case scenario. The history of your species so often opting for less impactful solutions, or disavowing any solution be needed — opting out — is proof enough for us that your planet will almost surely continue to heat up long after 2050. Maybe you'll self-immolate. We'll leave the apes to watch you burn.

This matters enormously to us since we must "sit back" and witness your slow churn into suicide. You already know this, deep down. You can feel the quakes in your soles, the sizzle in the air, the vibration from the oceans whipping themselves into pulsars without the benefit of magnetic braking. You know, but you've forgotten. Or maybe it's a willful turning of blind eyes and deaf ears. The lighthouse beams into the unused corners of your brains. Unobservable parts of the universe.

This has all been said. Our hope is that with repetition the message will get through. Often it doesn't. It's like a motif in poetry that no one's read. We've read it countless times in your own history. It's starting to get boring.

The backpacker had loaded his pack with five clean t-shirts, an unopened container of nuts, a pair of nail clippers, and the handwritten addresses and phone numbers of two homeless shelters. He went to where he'd met Tanner, but Tanner wasn't there. The backpacker despaired. His pack was heavy with all the things he needed to give away, as well as with his writing materials, laptop, earbuds, charger, et cetera spinning et cetera.

Tanner was not to be found. Maybe he'd disappeared. Turned to a wisp and been blown down an unnamed alley.

This matters to us.

The backpacker lugged himself and his laden pack in ever larger rings round the epicenter of where Tanner had once been. He'd witnessed an abundance of homelessness, but he couldn't find Tanner. The backpacker's despair deepened.

We'd watched this unfold since we knew it all mattered.

On a bench, separate from the rest of Doverton's downtown homeless, Tanner slept on a bench facing an empty bench across from him. Since his eyes were closed, the fact that the bench opposite had been empty may not have mattered in the least to him, but the fact that the bench he'd been in was occupied by himself, the much sought-out Tanner, was of enormous importance to the backpacker.

We knew what was going to happen. This is one of the many reasons we watch. Like a television show even though you know they'd never completed the series., the finale still in a document on a laptop in the dark corner of the unobservable universe. Or else sucked into a blackhole.

Television doesn't matter to us. It's one of your many drugs. Species like yours, however, are our television, our entertainment.

We hate to tell you this. We know how unshakeable your species' faith is in itself. You think you matter. More than anything.

It's true, for you, of course. But whether you're actually right or wrong—straight-faced staring or vibrating in delusion—the very fact of you, of your existence, matters to us more than you'd ever believe possible of cosmological energy.

No, we're not God. Don't confuse the semantics. Go back and read those scientific papers of climate change. Leave the gods in the gathering clouds over the oceans.

We are dark energy. We aren't dark energy. They're your terms, so they don't fit as snugly as the backpacker's t-shirt he's wearing. They hang off us like the given tees will hang off Tanner's gaunt frame.

This part, this part right here, matters. Pay attention.

Reluctant to wake him, the backpacker called Tanner's name nonetheless. Maybe he didn't want some other poor beggar to make off with Tanner's recently acquired goods. Grave goods. But Tanner woke up. He was groggy with resurrection. The backpacker stated each item as he laid them on the bench or handed them directly to Tanner.

Here are some shirts. Can you use shirts? They're clean.

Here are some nuts. A whole container.

Here are some clippers.

These people here can help you find a place to stay and they're not too far away.

The backpacker handed Tanner the slip of paper.

Tanner seemed thankful, yet still groggy.

It was hot this day, too. Just like the first time the backpacker had met Tanner.

Take care, the backpacker said.

We wish energy could weep, for we would weep.

The backpacker put his pack back on. It was lighter. A weight lifted. He walked down the street. He got three blocks away and the back of his right hand shot up and pressed against his right eye.

The backpacker wept.

Energy can weep after all, for we wept, too.

This matters so much, and it pains us to know that you'll most probably miss the point.

Not everything has a resolution. Not every tale. Some have an even mixture of good and bad. Some worse, some better than others. Sometimes nothing happens at all. Life can lead to non sequiturs. Life can hand you a lemon and the lemon only. Lemons to lepers with atrophied muscles. Life can hand you the lemon press, grant you crushing thews, and deny you the lemon. It can set a wet dripping glass of freshly-squeezed lemonade on the porch table. Maybe you're not there, hadn't seen it. Maybe you don't even have a glass. Maybe all that willful blindness has obfuscated any sweet gift granted. It'll melt on the porch table. Rings will form. The clouds over the oceans set themselves into spins.

Sometimes it rains and you get wet. No one cares whether you've got an umbrella or not. They're not watching you and you're not watching them.

We're watching, though. It hardly matters to you, we know, since we also know that we—being disembodied energy—couldn't, and never would matter to you.

Yet we never stopped watching.

Why?

It's not merely entertainment. We can't tell you the real reason. You must discover that for yourselves.

Or else drown in your own lungs.

Burn up with your planet.

Float like bloated ticks in the tears of the Earth that you'd forced out.

This is the most important part. This is the thing that matters the most. This is a moment in a long chain of moments that you've ignored for too long.

The apes shuffle and peek through the green canopy. They grunt. Something's happening.

It doesn't matter, you say. We're all going to die, anyway.

And what?

Find a new Earth?

Attain enlightenment?

A paradise with seventy-two virgins?

How? Through indifference? Through violence? With blind eyes and deaf ears?

We've already said this. Repetition. Poetry. You're still not listening.

The reason it matters that you figure it out for yourselves why we're watching is the most important thing in your backwatered, observable universe. Every species must come to this self-realization or expire. You are not unique.

You're on the edge of extremism and extermination.

Cry and wail. Throw rocks and missiles. Tell us to shut the hell up, already.

None of it will matter.

We're energy. We can't feel a thing. We can't even properly weep.

So, have you figured it out?

Don't worry. We'll give you time. You've got until at least 2050.

We can hear the fatalists say that none of this matters. Not even the fact that we've stepped in and tried, and probably failed, to speak to you. We pushed matter to be here, to be here now, and you've stopped up your ears.

Oh, stiff-necked apes.

Don't be flippant. Don't be glib. No one's coming to take your jobs or guns or land or money or cars or sneakers or wives or husbands or children or planet. Not now. You know this.

You've done this to yourselves, and we watched it happen, all the way from apedom. You've prepared for enemies that never existed. You've been restless in your invention.

Evolved from grunts, devolved into grunts.

Rev the gas in your big, big trucks. Yank back on the throttles to the jet skis. Fly halfway round the world to save relationships that could've been fixed in the backyard if you'd only had the damn will.

Do you have the will? We mean, to stave off disaster?

Not even half of your richest country is vaccinated, and they could've got the shot free, while the poorest parts of your world suffer. It's your privilege, we understand. Shooting guns is way cooler, anyway.

Turn a blind eye.

For every season.

Turn a deaf ear.

We, if anyone, know how true it is to say that there's nothing new under the sun. Under any sun, not just your middling twinkler. Preach on, poor beggar, preach on!

Your rights, your God-given rights. The right god. The boots you've had the poorest of the world manufacture halfway across the world. They don't fit, you complain, and so you return them to the warehouse. Another pair is shipped out, woven and glued by other poor fingers. You put them on and strut about and use the heels of those new boots to place on the cracks of pavement, the necks of the weakest of your species. Now how are those fingers going to sew?

We've seen species like yours die off before. Better species, even, further advanced. In other solar systems, other galaxies. Not just civilizations. Whole planets. Confederations of planets. The one commonality—like the unclipped nails of the homeless—is that they did it to themselves. There's rarely a random solar flare or gamma ray burst. Those astronomical events usually only incinerate already dead planets.

You did this. We watched it happen.

Does it matter yet? Have you figured out yet why we're here?

We were once matter, too.

There's a hint.

We're still here.

Get your shit together.

This matters whether you want it to matter or not. Your unflappable belief is so banal.

Tanner will put on a fresh t-shirt.

This will matter.

The backpacker will make it a lifetime goal to help those in need.

This will matter.

Spouses will speak with each other in their backyards and repair what's broken.

This will matter.

Someone will choose not to pick up that gun and randomly shoot at a house.

This will matter.

Someone will ruin their brakes and not crash into another human.

This will matter.

Someone will go to a funeral because they'll want someone to go to their own funeral.

This will matter.

The person who was paid to assassinate another person decides to not go through with it after all. The money doesn't matter.

This will matter.

Poetry from beggars will be heard by strangers.

This will matter.

You'll know exactly where you are and where you should be and can name the names of all the many alleys.

This will matter.

A couple will learn they don't need to join a club to stay in love.

This will matter.

And maybe some people will learn to not hate others just because they're different. They'll sit down and talk. They'll brave the offensive smell of the homeless, the offensive rhetoric of the opposing party. The lion will lay down with the man and woman as the lamb skips away.

We don't know how else to say it. Your own species, members of your own race, have written longer tales that have said the same thing we are now. It's nothing new.

Not even the sun. It's of middling age. There are older suns. There are bigger suns.

We'll be here always, watching. Never fear.

This — this fact of our observation will matter more than you'd imagine.

And when the full light of comprehension hits you — if it ever does, if you find yourselves so blessed to bless yourselves with the gift of understanding — you'll see that this is true. That it matters.

That it all fucking matters.

Otherwise, we'll just watch another sad televised series of a species' self-constructed demise.

Man, that sucks.

It hurts to see it. It always does.

It's not entertainment.

It's the saddest story in the universe.

Please don't put us through that again.

Please we beg please please.

Figure out why it all matters.

There's nothing else that does.

Not even for us.

...ACKNOWLEDGEMENTS...

To Kim for the editing.

To the wife for the layout and cover art.

To Tanner and the other homeless persons I met along the way.

All good representatives of TEAM HUMAN.

This beggar thanks you from the bottom of his heart.

HOBO CODES

Safe camp	Man with a gun lives here	The sky is the limit	This way
You'll be cursed out	Dangerous neighborhood	Kind woman (Tell sad story)	No use going this way
If you're sick, they'll care for you	Easy mark, sucker	Hoboes arrested	This is the place
Good road to follow			

Source: www.quora.com/Are-hobo-signs-still-in-use
Also see: #TBT – Hoboes, bums, tramps: How our terminology of homelessness has changed - National Coalition for the Homeless (nationalhomeless.org)

Made in the USA
Columbia, SC
11 July 2024